LACE

LACE

Catrin Kean

HONNO MODERN FICTION

First published in Great Britain in 2024 by Honno Press
D41, Hugh Owen Building, Aberystwyth University, Ceredigion, SY23 3DY

1 2 3 4 5 6 7 8 9 10

A catalogue record for this book is available from the British Library.

Published with the financial support of the Books Council of Wales.

ISBN 978-1-912905-74-4 (paperback)
ISBN 978-1-912905-75-1 (ebook)
Cover design: Ifan Bates
Text design: Elaine Sharples
Printed by: 4edge Limited

This is a work of fiction and no resemblance to persons living or dead is
intended or implied.

To Fizzy,
My brilliant friend

This is a work of fiction. But my grandmother – Mary – did spend much of her childhood in a Dublin orphanage. The trauma of it remained with her for life. This book is for her – and for the many others.

'Although the wind
blows terribly here,
the moonlight also leaks
between the roof planks
of this ruined house.'

Izumi Shikibu

CHAPTER ONE

milk

She is born in the time of the yellow leaves falling: a tiny thing, curled like a secret; a creature who stares at shadows.

'I'm calling her Teresa,' Mary tells Louis after the midwife has left and Ellen is downstairs boiling the bloodied sheets in the scullery. Named after her favourite sister. 'You want to hold her?'

But Louis just wants to gaze, to cup his hand over her dark head, to marvel at her fingers and toes, her nails like jewels and her ears like seashells. The smallness of her: the completeness. The baby-skin scent of her. Mary wonders whether he is disappointed she isn't a boy.

After she arrives the air in the house shifts, as though someone has thrown open a window. Mary lies in bed listening to the comings and goings of neighbours bringing gifts, to Ellen singing to herself, and later, to Louis and Noah getting a little raucous with a bottle of rum. Night mist curls around the streetlamps outside, and yellow light breaks through the lace curtain and splinters on the floor. The baby makes little mammal sounds as she sleeps and expressions flit across her face, brief as a cloud crossing the sun. Mary watches her and watches her, trying to know her. She has waited for this child for a long time, this blending of hers and Louis' blood, this affirmation of their union. There have been many disappointments over the years, some just a speck of blood on her underclothes, others something more awful, something best not to look at: fairy children who didn't want to stay. For three days and three nights she watches the face of her longed-for child and tries

1

to feel something. Ellen comes and goes with an endless supply of freshly washed nappies and trays of bread and dripping, bowls of stew, glasses of Guinness. 'For the milk.' Louis even brings tea – Louis, who sits an arms-reach from the kettle and calls her away from whatever she is doing to take it off the boil. The midwife comes, pokes and peers at Mary to see how she is healing, and then whisks the swaddled baby downstairs for a bath in the sink, where the complaints from her tiny lungs can be heard all along the street. On the third night, as the foghorn calls from the sea with its mournful moon-voice, Mary feels the flood of milk in her breasts, and something else moving inside her too. She starts to cry and can't stop. She cries for the whole world, for the terrible place she has brought the child into.

But most of all she cries because she can't love her.

'Oh, the floodgates have opened,' says Ellen, offering a handkerchief. 'It's perfectly normal.' She tells Louis to stay away, to leave Mary to weep herself dry.

'She'll feel better in the morning.'

But birthing a child is like a tide flooding in. And tides uncover things that would have been better to have remained hidden.

CHAPTER TWO

sea-smoke

When Mary Byrne was six years old her mother slammed the front door of their cottage behind them and hoisted her children into the back of a cart to start a new life in the city.

Sea-smoke spun in, creeping along the harbour wall. Three-year-old Aggie wailed, her face snot-wet, and Mary's older sister Nora held her tight, whispering songs into her hair. Mary and Tess held hands under the blanket, their cloud-breath mingling. James sat with his back to all of them, pretending not to cry.

Neighbours watched from doorways, arm-wrapped against the cold. Mammy flung her shawl over her head and climbed up beside the driver, straight-backed.

'Small town people,' she said. 'It'll be different in the city.'

She nodded to the driver. He slapped the reins on the back of the sad, hunched horse and they set off, away from the cottage on the harbour where Mary had slept in a bed under the eaves with a tangle of sisters for the whole of her life, where she had felt safe until the day that she'd seen Daddy laid out on the kitchen table in his British Army uniform, his face cold as a rock.

The cart rattled along the harbour wall, away from the stacked fish baskets and the herring boats with their rigging webbed against the sky; away from the calls of the boatmen and Mad Maggie's blasphemous songs. They crossed the river bridge and lonely birds called across the water, the church looming on the hill above them. Somewhere behind it, Daddy slept in the earth.

Hardly anyone came to Daddy's funeral: just a handful of

neighbours and the lodgers, three sea-scented harbour labourers who slept in the second bedroom, packed like fish in the small bed with their grime-soled feet poking out from under the blankets. Aggie cried but nobody else did. Mammy's face was as grey as the ashes the priest spoke about.

In the days after the funeral Mammy had a lot of whispered conversations with Kathleen Brien, one of the few neighbours still speaking to them. The children knelt on the floor of the bedroom, peering through the cracks between the floorboards, trying to decipher the low voices of the women. It was after one of these conversations that Mammy burst into the bedroom as they pretended to sleep.

'Get up. Get your coats.'

A wind whipped in from the sea, cold and breathy. Mammy walked fast up the hill towards the church, the children in a silent little line behind her. The church was in darkness, solid and watchful. Mammy hammered on the tall door with both her hands.

After a long moment, someone unbolted the door from the inside. It creaked open, just a little, and Father Patrick peered out, at Mammy, at the cluster of children behind her, then stepped backwards into the dark chasm of the church. They followed him.

Mary had never seen the church like this: stone-cold and silent, no curls of incense smoke, no crying babies, no stained-glass saints. The only lights were from the prayer candles. Father Patrick's face was shadowed, unreadable.

'Please,' said Mammy. 'I need help. I have no food, no money for the rent.'

Mammy, who was proud, who never asked for anything.

'Your husband was a weak and foolish man,' said Father Patrick, and an echo came back: 'man, man.' Mary felt the blind eyes of the saints watching them.

'He had his reasons, Father. He didn't want his family to starve.'

The flicker of a smile appeared on Father Patrick's face, then died.

'And is any of it my fault?' Mammy said. 'Is it the fault of the children?'

4

There was a long silence, and then Father Patrick turned and walked away, his cassock flying around his ankles.

'Father, please...'

The voice came out of the blackness.

'Ask the British Army for help.'

Daddy had sold his fishing boat and joined the British Army. He was going to Africa to fight the savages, he said: he would get a good pension, he said. But he had only got as far as England before he fell ill. They delivered him back in a box.

According to the British Army, the family weren't owed a farthing.

At the far end of the church an unseen door creaked open and then slammed shut: the prayer candles shuddered.

Mammy turned, dipped her fingers in the font, made the sign of the cross and left. The children followed, afraid to say anything, afraid that something terrible was about to happen.

And it did. Mammy sat on the steps of the church and sobbed.

Mammy had buried her husband and a drowned son without weeping. Mammy had held her head high when neighbours had shouted at her in the street, that the family were traitors and Unionists. Mammy was six feet tall and as strong and unbreakable as the ruins of the Black Castle which stood, impervious on the rocks above the town, enduring centuries of storm rage.

But now she had crumbled, which meant that the world had ended.

Nora shook her shoulder. 'Mammy stop it, mammy get up!' The other children just stood and stared in horror. Somewhere, a dog howled and men's voices floated up the hill from the harbour: a late fishing boat coming in. Yellow leaves spun and scuttered.

Then the church door creaked open again and Father Patrick came out. He handed Mammy a letter and without a word went back inside again. Mammy wiped her eyes with the back of her hand and read it. There was a long pause. Then she folded it, sniffed, and stood up.

'Let's go home.'

Three days later, they left, taken away by a rickety cart pulled by a bony old horse. Away from the fish-scent, from knees bloodied in rock scrambles. Away from the pockets full of shells and the mermaid stories the sisters told one another. Away from the sleep-tangled bed and the shards of light between the floorboards as Mammy made lace late into the night. Away from the warm smoke-crackled kitchen, away from the slap of the sea against the harbour wall and the seabirds keening: the song of their dreams.

Away. Daddy's old dog, who had been scavenging in the alleyways, appeared in the road in front of them. He moved aside to let the cart pass, sniffing the air, confused. Then he realised: they were leaving him. He ran after them, biting at the wheels, barking into the fog. Mary put her hands over her ears and eventually he slowed, stood watching them go, and he and the cottage and everything were lost in the sea-smoke.

CHAPTER THREE

the fair city

Mary curled into Tess's bony warmth and tried not to think of the dog or Daddy or anything, and eventually she fell into an icy, dreamless sleep to the rocking rhythm of the cart. She awoke to Tess shaking her.

'Look!'

They were in the city, and it was lovely as a fairytale, with lit-up buildings as high as the sky and everything reflected in the river. The children got onto their knees and stared: and look at that, and that, and that. There were people everywhere, and horses and carriages, and motorcars, and trams. Messenger boys on speeding bicycles. Smoky warm-lit pubs.

'D'you think there are princesses here?' asked Tess. They saw a lady with feathers in her hat. Maybe she was one.

'We'll be staying with my husband's cousin,' said Mammy, and showed the driver a piece of paper with an address on. The driver nodded without looking at it: he hadn't said a word for the whole journey and seemed as sombre as his horse.

They arrived at a large terraced house behind iron railings on a street lined with trees that held clenched fists up to the sky. Mammy lifted the children out one by one: their bodies were stiff as dolls. They stood shivering on the pavement while Mammy paid the driver.

'It's a fine house, for sure.' Mammy smiled, took a breath and then pushed open the creaky gate.

'Are we going to live here?' asked Tess. Mary couldn't imagine living in a house so large. Wouldn't they get lost? Mammy rapped the brass door knocker which was in the shape of a lion's head.

'Sssshh,' said Nora, who had learned not to ask questions over the past few months, as there was either no answer or it was not what you wanted to hear.

After a few moments, a shadow darkened the reflected light in the glass, and a man opened the door. He had a sad melted face as though he had been made from wax. He stared at Mammy and her clutch of children.

'It's Jane,' Mammy said. 'Jane Byrne.'

A woman's voice called from somewhere in the house: 'Who is it?'

'It's Martin's wife,' he called. 'With the children.'

'We've had a bit of trouble,' said Mammy, and he nodded.

'I heard.'

He stared at them a moment longer as though weighing things up.

'What does she want?' called the voice.

'I want ... I came to ask...' said Mammy, suddenly faltering and uncertain.

'Excuse me.'

The man shut the door and went back inside the house. Mammy stared at the door. Please don't cry again, thought Mary.

They could see the silhouettes of two people nodding to each other behind the frosted pane of the door, like shadow puppets.

The door opened again.

'We'll take the boy,' the man said. 'He can make himself useful as a messenger.'

Mammy smiled, but then just as quickly the smile disappeared.

'I'm sure you could find a use for the girls too...'

'I'm sorry,' the man said, and his face melted downwards a little more. 'My wife has been sick. It's all we can offer.' He opened the door a little wider and nodded at James.

James turned to look at them all and Mary knew he wanted to cry. Mammy hugged him tight. 'God bless you,' she said to Daddy's cousin. Then she let James go. They watched as James picked up his

8

bag and went into the house. The door closed behind him and he turned to shadow.

Somewhere, a clock struck twelve.

CHAPTER FOUR

orphans

They walked and walked almost for ever, and the city lost its magic, grew colder and darker and quieter around them, until the only other living things were the wailing cats. Mammy carried Aggie on her hip, her little shawl-wrapped head bobbing, a flower on a stalk. Nora, Tess and Mary walked behind them. Nobody said a word.

At last Mammy said, 'We're here.'

At the top of a hill, behind a pair of wrought-iron gates, was a square, austere building. Its dark windows were barred, like the prison at home where the wicked people lived. To the side of the path that led up to it was a cemetery, yew trees arching their sad arms over the graves.

'Where are we?' asked Mary.

'This is the orphanage.'

Mammy put Aggie down and pushed open the gate.

'But we're not orphans.' Tess, her voice bubbling with panic.

The gravestones looked like people kneeling, praying, bent-necked and silent. As Mammy started to walk towards the building, Aggie pulling at her skirt and grizzling, Mary suddenly knew, without a shadow of a doubt, that the praying people were going to raise their heads as she passed. They already knew she was there: they had heard her coming.

She turned and ran, down and down the hill. She didn't know where she was going: anywhere there was light. Anywhere away from this darkness, from the praying dead people. But a hand gripped her arm, fingers digging through her coat into her flesh, pulling her back.

Mammy slapped her.

'D'you think I want to do this?' Mammy shouted. Her eyes were glittering and the skin under her eyes looked bruised.

'I will come back for you. I will.' Her grip loosened. 'You have to be brave.'

Nora, behind her, stepped forward and took Mary's hand.

'I'll help you. We can be brave together.'

Tess, her eyes as round as the moon, took Mary's other hand and squeezed it. Aggie sniffed, spread snot across her face with the back of her hand and took her mother's hand. And the five of them walked back towards the building holding hands: a string of beads. As they passed the graves they said the Lord's Prayer together, loudly, to drown out the voices of the dead people.

'F'rever and ever AMEN.'

Mammy rang the doorbell.

*

Mother Superior had pink, wet eyes like a baby mouse and her face looked as though it was crawling with tiny red spiders.

'These children are not orphans,' Mammy told her. 'They are my children.'

Mother Superior nodded. Waited.

'My husband died and left us penniless,' Mammy said, the faintest whisper of a tremble behind her voice. 'So I am going to train at the Dublin Metropolitan Technical School for Nurses. Here is my letter of recommendation.' She held out the letter that Father Patrick had given her. Mother Superior put on some metal rimmed glasses she'd been clutching in her hand and squinted at it.

'But I am not allowed to have the children there with me.'

They were standing in a shadowed, cavernous hallway, watched over by stone deities. It was colder inside than outside. Mother Superior folded the letter and handed it back to Mammy.

'I will return for them as soon as my training is done.'

'Very well,' said Mother Superior. 'Who have we here then?' Her teeth were loose and tinkled like old piano keys when she spoke.

'Nora, ten, Mary, six, Tess, five, and Aggie, three.'

Mother Superior clicked her fingers at the darkness at the edge of the hall and a nun materialised. She looked like she was made of mist and she had the face of a ghost. Sister Benedict flapped her hand over the heads of Mary's sisters.

'Take these three to their beds, please.'

'Come this way,' whispered the new nun, her voice thin as air. Mary took a step to follow them.

'No, no, not you.'

Mary looked at her mother, terror fizzing inside her.

'Can't the children stay together?'

'We place them in the dormitories according to age.' She smiled at Mary. 'Don't be worrying, we have plenty of friends for you.'

Nora, who was standing very straight-backed, took Aggie's hand, but Aggie threw herself around Mammy's legs and started screaming. No-no-no Mammy no. Mary thought, Mammy's going to realise this was all a mistake. We're going to walk away, find the man with the sad horse, and ask him to take us home again. But Mammy did nothing. She just stared at Aggie, frozen. Mother Superior peeled away her cold little hands.

'There, there, be a good girl now.'

Tess started crying too, but quietly, her fist stuffed into her mouth.

'There's no need for such a fuss,' whispered the shadow. She grabbed Aggie's wrist and the four of them walked away into the darkness, Aggie's head twisting back to stare at them, her mouth gaping and awful and her screams echoing up to the stone ceiling and all around, until they had all disappeared into the blackness and her screams were swallowed by the night.

Another nun stepped out of the darkness, as though this was a play and she'd been waiting in the wings. This one was smiling.

'You go with Sister Angelica now,' said Mother Superior. Mary looked at Mammy, hoping for a final reprieve. But Mammy's face was as cold and still as her dead husband's; the only thing alive about her were her hands which were fluttering open and closed like bird wings. She looked as though she didn't know who she was, or who Mary was, or anything.

No one was going to help.

Sister Angelica walked fast, her habit swinging around her ankles. She was pretty, with pink cheeks and dark-lashed blue eyes. If Mary and Tess were to put her in one of the stories they told one another she might have been an angel, like her name.

They walked through a labyrinth of dark corridors. Mary tried not to look into the shadows. She could hear whispers, as though the walls were praying. She could hear the saints breathing. She tried to keep the cloud of panic inside her head, because if it escaped she felt that it might destroy her and the whole place with it. They went down some stone steps that led to a heavy wooden door. Sister Angelica turned to smile at her.

Behind the door was the sound of dripping water.

CHAPTER FIVE

mermaid

When Mary Byrne was six years old she learned that fear is a shapeless thing, like water, filling every available space. As she lay in her bed in the dormitory, among rows of other beds, she felt it pushing against the walls and out through the cracks in the windows, flooding the world. She could see the shapes of the other girls lying shrouded on their backs with their hands crossed over their chests; little corpses. The room stank of urine.

Her brain span and spat like a Catherine wheel: James Mammy Nora Tess Aggie the dog, all lost in the night, all gone. She shut her eyes tight, trying to squeeze it all away, the horror of it.

And then she felt a hand grab hers, cold as a clam.

A girl stood by her bed. She looked as though she was made of silver: her skin gleamed and her eyes were the colour of water. Her pale hair was sheared short and uneven. At first Mary thought she was a ghost, but then she handed Mary something that may have been intended as a doll – a few sewn together pieces of material, a feather, a leaf.

'For you,' the girl said.

A shiver rustled the dormitory, as though by speaking the girl was committing a terrible sin.

'My name's Glennie,' said the girl, 'and my mother's a mermaid.'

*'When the netted fence of spiderwebs
that darkens my ruined house
can hold the wind in its strands –
that's when these troubled thoughts
will blow away...'*

Izumi Shikibu

CHAPTER SIX

moon jelly

In the old cottage Mary and Tess used to watch the sea for mermaids, so to meet an almost-one, a half-one, was thrilling.

She hasn't thought about Glennie for a long time. She locked her away behind that door in the back of her mind, never to be opened again. But as she sits by the window watching the night, the baby chomping on her sore nipples, the door is creaking open and things are spilling out.

When she was younger, when her mind was a fantastical world that hadn't yet been put in order, she'd imagine Glennie as a moon jelly, floating across all the seas of the world, with no separation between her and the seawater; no hard bone or edges, the ocean carrying her and she carrying all of the ocean within her.

But now she's an adult she knows this is childish fancy. Wherever Glennie is, she is hard bone and nothing else, bone crumbling to dust in some secret, unworshipped place.

The orphanage was so vast, the walls looming above her head right to the sky, the windows that admitted slats of cold light too high for her to look through; she felt as though she was an insect. The nuns glided through shadowed corridors, cold as statues, tall as the ceilings, but she was tiny, small as the snails who trailed slow silver trails behind them. It was a lovely thing, she thought, to carry your home on your back: you could go anywhere. When the children were made to go outside in the exercise yard, she wouldn't look at the out-of-reach sky, but at the snails, and the ants who lived in the cracks. Do they even see us, she wondered, or are we too big?

And does that mean there is something living above us too, so huge we don't even know it's there?

She asked Glennie what she thought.

'Mm,' Glennie said. She always said this when she was asked a question, as though it was very important and she had to think hard. She stuck out her tongue, lapped at the sliver of snot running from her nose, and squinted at the sky. Pondering.

'Mm. Well, they'd have to be so, so big that we can't see them.'

'But we are so, so big to the ants,' Mary said. 'I don't think they can see us either.' And the two of them squatted in the dirt and watched the ants in their tiny world in the crevices, oblivious to the giants above them.

Mary found this thought comforting, that they were all so tiny under the sky, because it meant nothing really mattered. Like the ants that were crushed underfoot and forgotten, so would it be for her, and her sisters, and Glennie.

She imagined that she and Glennie were spiders, weaving their silk webs behind a gossamer curtain, safe, silent, wreathing their threads in the dark.

Sometimes, deep in the night, Mary heard a bird singing, and she thought that was the saddest thing, to sing with no one listening.

The sisters were forbidden to speak to one another, but Mary learned to smile at them using just her eyes when she saw them across the cold refectory, or at Mass. Glennie taught her to avoid the hard eyes of the bully girls, empty as rocks, and not to look at the skinny babies with wrinkly skin and wailing gargoyle mouths in case they visited her in nightmares. She learned to scrub stairs and floors and not miss a bit lest the cane should sting the back of her knees, or worse, that she should be kicked down the stairs. Glennie showed her how to tip crumbs into her apron to have a little bit more to eat, and where to find the potatoes that had rolled from the grocery cart; they'd hide behind the kitchen wall to eat them, imagining they were the sweetest apples, which you could do if you closed your eyes and thought about it hard enough. She learned to curl up her toes to squeeze them into the too-small mismatched shoes that the charity people brought, and to dig a heel into her chilblains to numb the pain – a moment of pleasure before the heat throbbed back in. She learned that the blood bubbling up from red-raw skin tasted sweet after she'd scratched at it. She learned to sleep on her back with her hands on top of the covers even when it was so cold she wanted to curl into herself like a cat, so the nuns could check that none of the little girls in the morgue-like dormitory were touching themselves.

She learned to close her eyes tight shut at night so that she couldn't see all the lonely ghost children who came from the cemetery to stare at the still-alive children, and not to listen to the dead babies who, so the whispers said, the nuns had hidden in the walls.

She learned not to wait for Mammy because she had been told that Mammy was wicked and was not coming back, which must be true because otherwise why would she have left them here? And she learned that she herself was wicked and must pray for forgiveness though it would ultimately do no good.

But there was one thing she was unable to learn.

When she slept, she was back at the cottage by the sea. Sometimes it was a bad dream: her dead brother Michael, floating face down on the waves, his little clothes all bubbled up like a balloon, and Mammy wading towards him, her dress clinging to her thighs and her arms outstretched to pluck him out, to hold him to the sky, to will him alive again. A whole ocean of grief spilling from her mouth.

Sometimes the dreams were happy ones, running on the shingle with her sisters and her still-alive brother and her other brother and a dog. The sun dropped down over the sea, a golden ball, and the little fishing boats jingle-jangled and everyone was laughing. But then she'd hear a cry, and turn.

And Mammy would be stood by the cottage door, her face all cracked like a statue, and her mouth opening wider and wider and her cry like the scream of a storm and water spilling out, dark water, flooding from her mouth, flooding the beach, the town, the whole world, and Mary was beating her arms against the tide, trying to stay afloat, trying to swim back to Mammy, to dive into her gaping mouth to safety...

'Filthy girl!' Someone gripped her arm, fingernails in her flesh. She was pulled from her bed onto the cold floor. The water receded and she was back in the dark dormitory with the rows of silent, corpse-like children.

Mary Byrne couldn't learn how not to wet the bed.

Sister Angelica marched a bedraggled line of bedwetters to the bathroom where they stood in a shivering, naked line, hands covering their secret parts, and took it in turns to scrub themselves down with carbolic soap in an ice-cold bath. They were not allowed to gasp at the first shock of water, but they couldn't help it and so they got a welt across their backs, their blue bodies reddening, tiny drops of blood bubbling.

When it was Mary's turn she closed her eyes and crawled into her secret spider space as her teeth chattered like they were about to burst out of her mouth and the red soap burned her skin.

When they had pulled on their clothes over their clammy bodies, they had to strip their cots and carry the stained, stinking sheets through the refectory where the other children were waiting to eat; a shameful little parade watched by the coal-dead eyes of the bully girls, by the menacing eyes of nuns, by the painted eyes of disappointed saints. They carried their sheets through to the steaming laundry where Mary sometimes saw Nora who was all bones now, with her hair all shaved off and her skin red and sore, Nora who looked at her and knew what she'd dreamt; it was a comfort, to know that while she was forbidden to talk to her sisters, they shared one another's dreams. When Mary handed her sheets to Nora their fingers touched for a second under the piss-soaked cotton.

Mary was scared of the bigger girls, of the crusty sores at the sides of their mouths and their empty eyes and their red raw fists. She missed Tess, missed the whispered stories in the old bed tangled with sisters. But she had a protector: Glennie, who slept next to her, who gave her the strange doll, who the nuns said was feeble-minded and had a streak of the devil in her, the girl with the silver eyes and a constant shining streak of snot sliding from her nose.

When Mary was with Glennie, the bigger girls stayed away.

Mary didn't think Glennie was feeble-minded. Glennie told wonderful stories about the things she had seen: dragons and fairies and giants, and about her mother who lived in the Liffey and ate fish and birds' eggs. Her hair was seaweed and her teeth were pebbles, which was more exciting than Mary's mother who was just learning how to splint broken bones and slosh out bed pans.

Glennie said that one day she was going to run away so that she could go swimming in the river with her mother, maybe all the way to the sea. She said Mary could come with her and they'd all go for tea at Bewley's after, and everyone would stare because no one in the whole world looked like her mother, but her mother had lots of money so who cared. Mary was a little scared about the river part, but tea in Bewley's sounded lovely because Glennie said she could eat as much as she wanted. When they ate the crumbs they'd collected in their aprons they imagined them as slices of tart, hot and oh so sweet. Glennie showed her how to click her fingers for service, and Mary imagined the waitress hurrying over, a little flustered and ever-so-polite in her black-and-white uniform.

But Mary secretly knew that however wonderful it sounded, she'd be too afraid to run away.

Glennie had quick-silver eyes that were never still, that never looked at you directly but at somewhere inside her own head, into her own spider-space. Mary loved listening to Glennie, following her into strange and fantastic worlds, and it seemed Glennie loved to listen to her too even though the space inside her head was not as wonderful.

'I think I saw a mermaid once,' Mary told her. She was remembering sitting on the rocks with Tess, watching something break the surface out to sea, sun playing on its gleaming skin, lighting it up like a rainbow. A mermaid for sure, they'd said at the time. In the days when Daddy was a fisherman they'd lie in bed listening to him drinking with men downstairs, and sometimes the men spoke of mermaids, beautiful women who lured boats into rocks, who called men away from their wives, never to be seen again. Mermaids were enchanting and deadly, and visited the sisters in dreams.

'Do you think it was your mother I saw?'

'Mm,' said Glennie. She was silent for a moment, and then looked straight at Mary. She didn't often look directly at anyone.

She smiled.

'I think maybe it *was* my mother you saw,' she said.

At night, eyes closed tight so as not to see the sad, wan ghosts who wriggled through the walls to stare at the live children, Mary imagined she was back at the cottage. She wanted to remember everything – the click of the door latch, the creak of the stairs, the damp stains along the skirting boards, the little statue of Our Lady with her sad mouth like an 'oh'. Glennie liked to hear all about it.

'So what did it look like?'

A little white cottage joined onto another cottage where old Mrs O'Connor lived and potatoes growing deep in the wet earth in the garden and the dog barking at the wooden gate which hung a little wonky on its hinges and a river behind and a mountain and the sea in front with all the fishing boats.

'So what did it sound like?'

Like crackling wood and footsteps on tiles and giggling sisters and someone whispering and someone snoring and the wind rattling the windows. And like boats jangling in the harbour and Mad Maggie singing rude songs in the dark and the sea going 'sssshhh'.

'What did it smell like?'

Like smoke and bread and rain and fish and wet dog and Daddy's ale and sometimes flowers.

'What did it feel like?'

Like scratchy blankets and warm hair and bread in the oven and arms wrapped around you.

'Mm,' said Glennie.

Sometimes, after Mass on a Sunday, Mammy came to visit, and Mary and her sisters had to scrub their faces and necks extra hard and put on a nice coat and hat that Mother Superior kept for occasions such as this, and they sat together on a bench in the garden. Mammy always pretended she was very happy when she saw them.

'Guess how many pennies I have saved for our new home?'

'A hundred,' said Aggie.

'A million,' said Tess.

Nora just sighed, as though the thought of counting anything was too much, and Mary ignored the question. Mammy's stupid jar of pennies under the bed would never be enough to get them out of here. She wriggled onto the cold bench next to Tess and elbowed her. Tess giggled, a sweet gap-toothed smile. She elbowed Mary back. Mary wriggled her leg against Tess's leg and Tess wriggled back: bony knee against bony knee. Mary whispered 'I love you,' into Tess's ear and this time Tess threw her head out and laughed in delight, the sound of it lovely as a bell, and Mary kissed her cold cheek and then they sat quiet and close, feeling one another's warmth. It was a bit like the olden days but at the same time not at all like that, the sisters with their horrible scrappy hair and their cough-coughing and the rasping pain inside the cages of their chests. Nora's face was sad as the moon and when Mammy stopped pretending to be happy her eyes got all wet, worrying about the sores on the side of their mouths and their flaky skin, saying they needed to eat more, especially Aggie: 'Look how thin she is, look how pale, look at the half-moons under her eyes!'

Aggie, tucked under Mammy's arm, clinging on tight as though Mammy was a lifeboat out at sea.

Sometimes, in the exercise yard, Mary saw Aggie standing by the railings, and wailing, wailing, her small face white and wet and her mouth open and twisted like a gargoyle. If no one was looking Mary would approach her: 'Don't cry, Aggie.' Try and touch her through the railings. 'Please, don't cry.'

But Aggie wouldn't look at her. She was looking at a space a few feet ahead of her through the railings, a space inside her own head. Around her children played and nuns walked and no one noticed her at all, this little ghost-child in their midst. Mary sometimes wondered whether she was really there at all, but was just a spirit weeping into eternity.

She didn't tell Mammy this.

Neither did anyone tell Mammy that despite her begging them to eat more, there was no more food to eat, that there was always a little empty pit of pain in their stomachs that was never filled. When a new Bride of Christ was ordained the children were invited to watch the feast, sitting straight-backed in rows, spittle-mouthed and hungry as dogs as they smelled the aromas of honeyed mutton and plum pudding, as they watched the Bishop and the priests in their ornate cassocks, and Mother Superior and all the nuns gorging themselves, juice running from their stuffed-full mouths. This was how Mary imagined it was for James in his big house after he had done his chores, too; a small boy in front of an enormous steaming plate of food, like a character in a comic.

Once, only once, Mary said the thing that was on her mind, that was on all their minds: 'When can we come home?' And Mammy didn't know what to say and Nora poked her in the ribs and she said 'ouch' and then nothing more.

As the other girls watched through the barred windows, Mammy handed out pieces of apple cake. The taste of that cake made Mary want to eat it all at once, but she wanted it to last for ever too, so she ate it crumb by crumb, feeling the sweet bitterness melting on her tongue. Even before she took the first taste she was already thinking, soon this will be gone, which made her feel sad. How soon things became a memory: maybe it was better not to have nice things at all. She always saved a sliver of it for Glennie because no one ever brought her apple cake; she was always sombre and silent after Mammy's visits and sometimes she rocked and frowned and pinched at her skin until it bled. Mary hid a piece of cake away in her apron pocket for Glennie and tried not to cry when she thought about leaving Tess again, at not being able to feel her warmth or smell her skin or hear her tinkly giggle.

They all thought these were sad occasions. Nobody guessed there would be one that was much sadder.

CHAPTER SEVEN

heaven

Early in the morning they smelt clothes burning.

Nuns rushed along corridors swift as shadows, trailing clouds of incense behind them, and the orphanage was full of whispers that flew and grew until it was clear what was happening: the White Plague had arrived.

Consumption.

Some important looking men in suits, handkerchiefs over their faces, arrived for meetings, and after that the children were ordered to make the rooms even colder by opening the windows wide. Lessons were cancelled in favour of a strict regime of cleaning. And when the cleaning was done to the nuns' satisfaction the children were made to stand for long periods in the exercise yard and ordered not to spit. The infected children were hidden from view in an isolation ward at the back of the building.

A death-scent of carbolic and disinfectant hung in the air and the children's hands were red raw from all the washing. At night Mary prayed fervently: please God keep Tess safe and Nora and Aggie and Glennie, Amen.

But at the age of nine Mary Byrne discovered that prayers didn't work.

She was on her hands and knees scrubbing the floor of the dormitory when Mother Superior appeared.

'Child, you are to come with me.'

This was unusual. Usually one of the lower nuns were sent on errands. Mary stood up, started to lift the pail to take it and tip it away.

'Leave that. Fetch your beads.'

Mary took her rosary beads from under her bed and followed Mother Superior to her small cosy office that smelt of lavender and woodsmoke.

Without a word Mother Superior undressed Mary down to her underclothes and put on a black dress that was too small, then roughly pulled what was left of her hair into a plait. She put a hat onto her head and a black cape around her shoulders.

'Put thethe on.'

Mother Superior had lost some more teeth and the remaining ones danced in her mouth when she spoke and she said 'th' instead of 's'. She handed Mary a pair of shoes that for once matched, and when Mary slipped her feet into them there was enough room to wriggle her toes. She smiled and almost said thank you, but Mother Superior's pink face was stern and so she stopped herself.

But something was happening. Was she going home?

'Hurry up now. Your mother ith waiting.'

Mammy! At last she was going home! She followed Mother Superior out, looking down at the lovely shoes as she walked, admiring the sheen of them, listening to the click click they made on the floor. Where would they live? she wondered. The only house she had seen in Dublin was the one James was living in, so tall and vast. Would it be like that one? It would be like being a princess in a castle, and there would even be room for Glennie to come live with them too.

She had new shoes and she was going home.

They reached the entrance hall and there was Mammy, also all in black, and Nora, and Tess, who were dressed similarly to her. And James! It was like the most wonderful dream.

But then she realised. Someone was missing.

*

Aggie's coffin was tiny, weighing almost nothing at all. As she was lowered into the earth Mammy made little gaps: 'oh, oh, oh,' and James, tall now, held her arm as though to stop her falling into the grave with her daughter, and Tess and Mary held hands and wept quietly and Nora stood silent as a wraith. Afterwards a little wooden cross was placed on top of the bed of earth. 'Agnes Mary Byrne, aged 6 years.' There wasn't room for more. But at least she had her own grave, not like the graves that the children were sometimes made to visit on Sundays, with the long list of names of girls whom no one had come for. Mary imagined them squashed in like fish in a tin, with contorted faces. No wonder they wandered back inside at night.

But wouldn't Aggie be lonely here, all on her own?

The priest spoke about committing Aggie's soul to heaven and Mary squinted and tried to see it, a puff of smoke as brief as a candle, slipping up through the ground and hovering above them.

There were a small gathering of adults there: the family who had taken James in, and Mammy's sister who had gone to marry a farmer in Sligo a long time ago. She seemed angry: she gripped Mammy's arm and said, you'll be bringing the lot of them out in boxes if you don't sort this out, look at the state of them, and Mammy's sad expression turned to fury and she said, 'I am doing my best, Catherine! I am doing my best!' and shook her sister's hand off her.

When she got back to the orphanage Glennie was waiting for her. Glennie hugged her and said 'Your sister's in heaven now, lucky thing,' and Mother Superior asked for the shoes back, and everything went back to how it was, and Mary even saw Aggie sometimes, playing with the other children in the sunlight.

She wasn't crying any more.

CHAPTER EIGHT

midnight

It's in the nighttime that the town's heartbeat comes alive, no longer muted by the rumble of trams and the click of footsteps and all the voices. It thrums from deep in the earth, and its voice is the songs of little coal trains as they move endlessly back and fore from the valleys to the sea, and the grinding of metal in the foundries, and the beat and throb of machinery and cranes, and the ships who call to one another with their lonely voices as they wait to be loaded, waiting to travel across the seas to all the world, to places where the sun is shining, to places where the light is the colour of pearls and gold.

Because the sun is always shining somewhere.

But not here.

The ships glide around the blue globe leaving shivery white trails behind them, moving through the vast expanses of water between lands, and somewhere on one of those lands is a tiny house lost in a vast world and that is where Mary lies.

She watches the watery pools of light and shadow shivering on the ceiling, as behind the curtains the rain skitters sideways across the window pane. A metallic drip, drip, drip beats a rhythm and water sings in the drains.

Sweet little Aggie.

She feels as though there are spiders under her skin.

She wants to slap Louis, who is sleeping the sleep of the innocent beside her, his breath making curdling noises in his throat. Sometimes he cries and shouts at night, but by the morning he has folded up his fears and put them away again, neat as sheets.

She can't lie still any longer. She gets out of bed, finds her slippers with her feet, throws on her dressing gown and lifts the baby out of the cot, a little too roughly; her black eyes jerk open wide in surprise.

It is that time that is furthest from dawn, and the only creatures awake are Mary and the mice. She takes the baby downstairs to the lean-to beside the kitchen. The dog, lying in the ashes in front of the range, stretches when she comes in and follows her.

When she arrived, in the middle of all that mayhem and hate, the lean-to was neglected and laced with cobwebs. She cleaned it, filled it with ferns, some she found herself and some that Noah brought her, and made it hers. She needed a place to work, she said. She set up her sewing table and sat there making curtains and tablecloths, cushion covers and bedspreads, under the shimmying shadows of the ferns. Bent over her machine she could hide the fact that she didn't have much to say to anyone: she could pretend that she would have had plenty to say, were she not so busy.

The rain drums on the glass roof and blurs the sky. She unbuttons her nightdress and pushes a nipple into the baby's greedy mouth and she suckles, making contented little noises. As Mary looks down at her dark curly head she thinks, how easy it would be to poke through the soft spot at the top of her head, right through to her brain. Like sticking your thumb in a pie. And then she cries, silently. Where did these wicked thoughts come from? What did this child do to deserve such a mother?

She can't even confess these things to the priest.

The baby's hot head bobs as she falls asleep again. Mary puts her in the basket and then stands there, not knowing what to do. She feels as though there is another Mary inside her threatening to burst out, a, dangerous creature who would slap her husband and burn the house down and throw her child into the Taff. She misses her job – the hushed, church-like basement where they worked, the low murmur of gossip, the scent of the fabric, the cutting, pleating, stitching; the finished dresses wrapped and hanging like ghosts, waiting.

34

But to go out to work is out of the question now.

Ellen has come downstairs; Mary hears her in the kitchen making tea. Ellen doesn't sleep well either; her aching bones wake her, so she wanders the house at night and whispers to herself; mad as a bloody hatter that woman is, though Mary keeps this thought to herself. Sometimes Ellen talks to the man in the photograph on the mantelpiece, Samuel, the black man with the narrow half-smiling eyes who had been her husband and Louis' father. But Mary and Ellen never speak to one another at these times, these two insomnious women watching shadows in their heads.

Sometimes, when the house feels too empty and too silent, she takes the baby into the front room and plays the piano, and the tunes spill through the walls and the house breathes again. But only when no one is home, as the piano is Louis' domain. Now, to calm herself she starts to tidy – wiping the fern leaves, dusting cobwebs that have gathered in the corner, giving the spiders time to skitter away before demolishing their homes. Then she opens the sewing box, starts pulling things out – ribbons and offcuts of brocade, reels of thread and balls of wool – such a mess, she thinks.

And then she sees something right at the bottom of the box. Something she'd quite forgotten.

A lace-making cushion.

CHAPTER EIGHT

wound

Every day was the same. They prayed, washed, prayed, had lessons, scrubbed floors, were beaten, prayed. But sometimes something happened that made things a little different.

After morning prayers, Mother Superior said something exciting was happening: they had a very important visitor. Behind her stood the prettiest lady Mary had ever seen, even prettier than Sister Angelica, with a small, smiling mouth and narrow smiling eyes and dark hair curling from under a velvet hat the colour of the priests' wine.

'Pleathe welcome Mithith Arabella Clayton,' said Mother Superior.

'Thome of you will thpend the day with her, instead of going to clatheth.'

There was a flutter of excitement in the hall, which died quickly as Mother Superior raised the part of her pink face where her eyebrows should have been.

'When I call your name you will come to the front.'

This in itself was strange: the children were never called by their names. Mother Superior scanned the room.

'Mary McCarthy. Annie Hickey...'

Mary waited as girls' names were called out. Please, pick me, she thought: please.

'...Agneth Farrell, Glennie Othaughnethy...'

Glennie gripped Mary's hand under the table before standing up. Mother Superior seemed to have finished. But then she looked straight at Mary.

'And Mary Byrne.'

Mary remembers it now, the excitement at being chosen.

But before that, something else happened. Glennie did what she always said she was going to do: she ran away.

'Come with me,' she begged, but while Mary was happy that Glennie was going to see her mother, she was afraid if she came too she would never see her own mother again, as she couldn't swim. They hugged, and cried, and promised never to forget one another, and promised they'd see one another again, and then Mary let her go.

Glennie had it meticulously planned out.

Early on a Friday morning the fish cart came bringing baskets of herring from the market. At breakfast on that day, Glennie took a mouthful of the thin grey gruel that passed as porridge and started shrieking and waving her arms around. Nuns descended: silence and contemplation was demanded at meal times. Glennie stood up, eyes wide, her hand over her mouth, retching.

Mary, afraid, kept her eyes on her bowl. Mother Superior stood up at the far end of the refectory, ready to admonish anyone who reacted. A flustered nun ushered Glennie out of the door while a frowning Mother Superior watched.

Mary heard the heavy door slam behind Glennie and then she was gone. She listened for the cart – the horse's metallic hooves taking Glennie away – but couldn't hear it through the thick walls. She imagined Glennie clambering into the cart. Would there be space under the baskets to hide? Would the fishmonger find her? Thinking about it all made Mary feel as sick as Glennie had pretended to be.

But she heard no shouting, no angry fishmonger voice ordering her out.

Mary tried not to cry as she thought of the horse taking Glennie away, away, down to the river, to her waiting mother. She thought of her as she scoured the pots and bowls after breakfast, as she scrubbed the floors. She thought of her in lessons, as she drew letters on her chalkboard. She thought of her at exercise time, missing her stories, her strange observations.

But then she saw her.

Mary was sitting alone in the exercise yard, an ice-wind, blown up from the Liffey, spinning round her in small tornadoes of dust. She was thinking about Glennie and wondering whether she was warm, when she saw her walking back up the driveway, a police constable holding firmly onto her collar. Mary thought she was imagining it at first but no, it was really her. Mary hung onto the railings while the other girls jostled around her, jeering and shouting until they were all ordered inside by a nun.

Mary waited for her that night, wanting to hear what had happened. Did she see her mother before she was caught? What was it like out there in the city – was it as sparkly as Mary remembered, the night they arrived? Did she have cake and lemonade in Bewleys?

But that night, and the night after, Glennie's bed was empty. She must have been put in the isolation room, which Mary had never been sent to but which was notorious: no light, no bed. Just a pitch-black stone cell. Mary prayed to God and the Virgin to keep her safe and to keep the ghosts away from her in the dark.

Very late on the third night, the dormitory door opened and the silhouette of a nun appeared in the dim light from the corridor pushing a small figure in front of her, before pulling the door shut again. The figure shuffled stiffly across the floor.

Mary smiled to herself in the dark and her belly constricted with excitement: she was back.

Glennie sat on the edge of her bed but didn't get under the covers. Mary waited for her to whisper something, and when she didn't, Mary went to join her on her bed.

'Did you see your Mammy?' Mary whispered.

Glennie was shivering so hard her teeth were chattering, and she was staring straight in front of her, shadows in her silver eyes. Without looking at Mary she indicated towards her back with a shaky hand.

Very gently, Mary pulled up Glennie's nightdress. And saw a pattern of dark stripes, intricate as the coat of a tiger, stinking of pus and blood. They were darker and deeper than those left by a cane or a belt: something red-hot and heavy had left these.

Mary spat onto her hands, and very gently placed her wet fingers into the wounds. Glennie shivered, but then settled, her breathing slowing a little.

Then she spoke, her voice raspy.

'I'm going to kill Sister Angelica.'

Mary felt a collective shudder rustle the dormitory but she knew that no one would tell. She stayed touching Glennie's wounds late into the night, and felt as though she was reaching straight into her heart.

CHAPTER NINE

lace

It became the best day of the week. The chosen girls sat at tables laid out in rows in a bright room with a wide fireplace where a fire was lit on cold days in case Mrs Clayton caught a chill. Stained glass windows sprinkled rainbows across the room. On each table was a small cushion, a ream of thread, a bowl of pins and some wooden objects that looked like hair grips.

Mrs Arabella Clayton was teaching them how to make lace. It would help their future job prospects, she told them, as well as maybe securing them a husband. The latter was especially thrilling, though none of the girls could really imagine that such a thing existed for them beyond these walls.

Mrs Clayton spoke like an English lady and in the rainbow light she looked even prettier.

Arranging the bobbins was a rhythm that made Mary's mind go quiet: over and under and under and over, securing the thread with pins so it didn't unravel, until she was ready to cut the piece of lace free, and there it was, a little piece of magic, not just an arrangement of threads any more but something else altogether. Something that had come from her. Mrs Clayton said they could make anything they wanted while they were learning, so Mary made shells, like the ones she and her sisters had collected on the beach and arranged on the cottage window sills.

Glennie worked with her face close to the cushion, eyes squinting in concentration, her snot-sucking tongue out. She said she was making a mermaid but it didn't look like a mermaid, it looked like

41

nothing at all, but before the classes Mother Superior had whispered to Mrs Clayton that she thought someone must have dropped Glennie on her head when she was a baby as she Wasn't All There, so Mrs Clayton was very kind and didn't say anything, just raised her pretty eyebrows a little and passed her by.

Making lace was like plaiting a sister's hair. In the lessons, to the quiet dance of the bobbins, Mary thought a lot about her sisters, who she missed so much it hurt. She thought about James, riding around Dublin on a bicycle with a basket, delivering messages, somewhere in the huge city beyond the wall. And she thought about Mammy who was out there too, learning how to be a nurse and saving up her money to rent a house to bring them all home. She remembered back in the cottage, peering through the bedroom floorboards watching Mammy in the kitchen below, her bent head in the candlelight, making pieces of lace to sell in the market. The children would go with her to help her set up her stall in the square, beside the sheep and horse traders, wool merchants, and herring and oyster fishmongers, hanging up baby shawls, wedding veils and tablecloths to drift in the brackish air.

Sometimes she thought about Daddy too, and sometimes those thoughts were bad ones, because if it wasn't for him they would still be living in the cottage with the sounds of seabirds and boat bells, but when she thought that she would whisper a sorry prayer into her rosary beads because God could hear everything you thought and would be angry.

And Aggie, little Aggie, who lay so alone under her wooden cross. Aggie with her sweet voice, who was always clinging onto someone's arm, twisting one leg behind her, thumb in her mouth. Who was looking after her now? When she thought of her the tears came suddenly, spilling onto the lace, warm and salty with sorrow. Glennie had told her that Aggie was somewhere lovely now, eating apple cake under a rainbow, or splashing in the bluest pool.

'She's in heaven,' Mary said.

'That is heaven, stupid.'

But the heaven in Mary's head didn't have such details – it was a vast and unknowable space – and she was starting to wonder whether Glennie really knew what she was talking about.

There was the future to think about too. Mrs Clayton had said if they worked hard there would be a husband and a job waiting. It was hard to imagine what her husband would look like as she didn't see many men, only the ruddy-faced delivery men with dirty fingernails whom she didn't fancy marrying, and the priests. But priests didn't have the private parts necessary for a marriage.

She wasn't sure what these parts might be but she had heard this from the older girls.

So a priest was out of the question.

In the end she fixed on the memory of a man she saw the night they arrived in Dublin: he had a sombre face and a top hat and looked, she thought, like a husband.

Mary had decided that lace, not Mammy's pennies, was her way out of here: those strands of thread were a rope that would allow her to escape to the world beyond the walls. But when she tried to talk to Glennie about it Glennie just rolled her eyes.

Mary thought Glennie wasn't helping herself at all. She was becoming ever more and more rebellious, almost as though she enjoyed the beatings which she was being subjected to more frequently. Her eyes had taken on a new glitter, as though she was getting some sort of thrill, as though she was goading the nuns to break her.

Mary was irritated at Glennie for not taking the lessons seriously; she was taking her strangeness too far this time. Her piece of lace was an ugly thing that looked nothing like a mermaid but more like some sort of ancient sea creature. She also stole pins and thread, squirrelling them away in her apron pocket, getting away with it because Mrs Clayton mainly ignored her.

At the same time Mary started to question Glennie's stories, those stories that used to entrance her. There was a lack of consistency, she realised. At first she had told Mary she had ten sisters, all of whom sat at the bottom of the sea eating fish. Mary started to doubt this story and one day asked her straight out: these ten sisters, what are their names? But Glennie denied ever having said it.

'I don't have any sisters, stupid.'

Then a brother appeared in the narrative, a little boy who had suffered a fate suspiciously similar to Mary's older brother Michael – toppling off a harbour wall and drowning, her mother diving in after him and becoming a mermaid.

She decided to do something about it.

'That doesn't look like a mermaid.'

'And how would you know? You never saw one.'

Mary didn't dispute this. With the benefit of age, she now thought that the creature she and Tess had seen may well have been a porpoise.

'Neither did you.'

'I did so.'

'I think,' said Mary carefully, 'you've been telling me fibs.'

Glennie's expression alarmed her with its cold fury, like a cloud had burst under her skin. But Mary pushed on.

'You're not going to get a husband and a job messing around and making up stories.'

'I don't want a husband and a job because then I'll be just like you. Stupid.'

And then she shouted again: 'STUPID!' Her voice bounced off the cold walls and a nun appeared from nowhere and grabbed her arm.

The nun swept away along the corridor, dark robes like a wing behind her, her fingers clawed into Glennie's arm. Glennie looked back at Mary and they kept their eyes locked until Glennie was pulled around a corner.

In the night Mary wanted to reach a hand out to touch her. But Glennie lay so silently that Mary couldn't tell whether she was awake or asleep. In the morning, when they made their beds, Mary wanted to throw her arms around her and say I'm sorry, I'm sorry. But

44

Glennie was faraway, somewhere in her head: it was as though she didn't know Mary was there, and Mary was afraid she didn't care about her at all, was afraid of Glennie looking right through her as though she was just air. They didn't speak for days, and Mary had a pain deep inside her heart because it was their first quarrel and it was almost the worst thing ever. Glennie blurred and softened the world: without her everything came into sharp, bitter focus.

It was Glennie who approached Mary at last, in the exercise yard, when Mary was drawing circles in the dust with her shoes.

'Look,' Glennie said, simply, as though nothing had happened between them. She glanced behind her to check that no one was near, and then she took her piece of lace from her pocket.

It still didn't look like a mermaid, but it looked more like something than before; it had a sort-of face with squinty button eyes. It reminded Mary of the doll-like thing Glennie had given her on the first night.

'This is Sister Angelica,' Glennie said.

She laid it on the ground and squatted over it. She took the stolen pins out of her apron and started to stab the doll, so hard that some of the pins bent. Mary was afraid.

'Glennie, stop it...'

Glennie ignored her; she carried on stabbing, her breath coming hard and angry. Stab, stab, stab: I hate her I hate her I hate her. The words forming spit and scattering.

And then a shadow loomed above them: a monolithic bird blocking out the winter sun.

CHAPTER TEN

for luck

This time, she never came back.

Mother Superior said that someone had allowed the devil to enter the building, which made the children shiver and say their prayers with added fervour, and hurry around shadowed corners in case there were demons waiting to steal them away in the dark. When Mary asked about Glennie they said her mother had come to fetch her home, and Mary believed this for a while, and imagined Glennie was happy, away from this place at last.

She wished they hadn't quarrelled during her last days there. She missed her more than she'd missed anyone. Even Mammy. Even Tess.

She empties out the basket but there's no thread. No bloody thread.

She knows she won't sleep tonight.

In the morning, after she has boiled a panful of nappies and hung them above the range, she swaddles the baby and pushes the pram through town, the wheels banging out a rhythm over the pavement cracks. It's cold – the sea blowing in a scent of snow. A woman in a fur collar stops to watch her and then comes over to the pram, smiling, her fingers clasped over the catch of her purse.

Mary smiles back.

The woman leans into the pram, recoils, then laughs.

'She's got a touch of the tar brush, hasn't she?' She pulls her fur collar closer round her neck and holds her purse close to her chest, as though Mary or the child were going to snatch it. Mary walks away, faster, towards the bridge.

'Stupid woman,' she says to the baby. 'What does she think you are, a doll or something? A stupid painted doll?' She looks behind her. She can't see the woman. Why does she always think of things to say after, when it's too late? She pushes the pram down the hill towards the bridge that has *BRAINS STRONG ALE* painted across its girder in large letters. A train is wheezing across, high above them, pulling wagons piled high with coal. Mary counts them: ten, fourteen, twenty-three. As she reaches the dripping gloom of the bridge the train is still rumbling over, rhythmic, filling the darkness with sound. The baby's eyes widen in fear.

'Whoop!' shouts Mary, over the sound of the train. Her voice echoes back at her – whoop, whoop – and the baby's eyes crease a little in a smile. By the time she emerges into the light again the train has passed over, is trundling away to the docks for the coal to be unloaded onto ships and taken to the far corners of the world.

She passes the pub, where a seaman and a woman are caught in an embrace in the open doorway. Mary smells hops and smoke through the open door.

She pushes open the door of the haberdashery shop and walks in, the bell announcing her arrival.

Dark, wooden floorboards. The scent of the fabric. The sharp-soft hiss of the scissors slicing through material as Ida serves a customer.

'What a lovely baby!' says the customer. Ida hands her a wrapped package, drops change in the till, and comes out from behind the counter, smiling. 'Oh, she's grown, Mary!' Ida looks thinner than ever. She is the same age as Ellen but looks older, with missing teeth and a map of her life scrawled into her papery skin. She bends over the pram and tickles Teresa under her chin.

Dolly comes through from the back of the shop, pins in between her teeth. Behind her in the back room stands a woman wrapped in royal blue material held together with pins. Dolly removes the pins from her teeth and puts them on the counter.

'I'll just be a minute,' Dolly says to the woman, and bends down

48

to Teresa. 'I've got a very important visitor. The prettiest visitor. The *prettiest.*'

Teresa stares at Dolly in wide-eyed wonder, her mouth moving as though she is trying to form words, to imitate Dolly, to reply.

'Clever too,' says Mary. 'She's nearly sitting up by herself now.'

Dolly was the result of a tryst between Ida and a handsome able body seaman from Jamaica, who boarded a ship to Brazil after three days of loving, never to be heard of again. Ida's Baptist family threw her out: to be an unmarried mother was bad enough, but for the baby to be 'coloured' was too shameful for words. Bringing up the baby alone was a struggle, but despite everything she still has a back as straight as a board, staring life full on even though it has punched her so many times. When Mary first met her she was afraid of her rough stare. But now she sees the kindness behind it.

'I've come to buy some thread,' she says. And while Ida and Dolly fuss over the baby, she pulls open oak drawers, fingers the little wooden reels of coloured thread, safe with these people who will not say anything stupid about tar-brushes.

Ida opens the till, takes out a threepenny piece and places it in the baby's palm, closing the tiny fingers over it.

'For luck, little one,' she says.

CHAPTER ELEVEN

dolly

Two weeks after arriving in Cardiff Mary received a note to say that her sewing machine had arrived at the port and was ready to be collected.

'We can arrange for that to be delivered,' said Louis. He was checking his reflection in the hallway mirror, preparing to go out on another job search. He was wearing his South Irish Horse uniform – dark green with red stripes and polished brass buttons. The uniform he was wearing when she first met him.

'Why don't you wear your Sunday suit?' she asked. And he turned to look at her, sharp.

'They have to know I served!'

It wasn't like Louis to snap – it jolted her a little. She reached up to adjust his cap. 'Very well.' She smiled, gave him a peck on his cheek, patted his chest.

'You look very handsome,' she said. 'Someone'll be sure to hire you.'

Louis – his burst of irritation already forgotten – winked, tipped his cap at her, and left.

Ellen was already in the shop, and Bright had gone, was goodness-knows-where by now, and Noah had left for work on a tramp steamer headed for Ireland.

Mary cleaned the grate and the dishes, swept the floor, beat the rugs, scrubbed the front step, then stood in the empty house listening to the arrhythmic sound of Louis' ticking clocks. There were other jobs to be done – polishing, dusting. She wasn't yet sure

51

what the division of labour was between her and Ellen, though she assumed, as she was the one left home, that the majority of it was to be done by her.

On the other side of the door was a town that had turned in on itself only a few days previously. But the anger seemed to have settled like ash – still there, but hidden in the cracks. If the rest of the family could venture out, then so could she.

And she didn't want to wait for her sewing machine to be delivered. She grabbed her coat and hat, checked her reflection in the blurred glass of the hall mirror, and left the house.

Outside Ellen's shop there were baskets of apples and strawberries that had been delivered by a farmer earlier that morning. She glimpsed Ellen through the glass, on her tiptoes, her arms upstretched putting something on a shelf.

She walked along the canal, dark water holding the green of the trees inside itself. Along the banks grew sprays of creamy meadowsweet, tall pink willowherb, enormous mallows with leaves as large as armchairs. A barge idled, a fisherman sat dreaming.

She stopped to look at the castle, at the brightly coloured coats of arms above its clock and the figures in their stone niches looking down at her. Behind, high on a mound, the old stone keep was suffocating in ivy like in a fairy tale.

She walked on – past inns, a laundry, fruit shops, a drug store. Past the indoor market with the scent of fish wafting out into the warm day. Past shouting newspaper hawkers.

She walked past alleyways that housed slums, where she hurried and kept her eyes down so as not to catch the eye of the weary women who leaned against doorways, or their spindle-thin children playing in the dirt.

On she walked, and on, through her new town – not as grand or expansive as Dublin, but with a bustle all of its own – blinkered horses pulling traps and carts, the rattle and whine of trams, the motorcars belching out clouds of stinking smoke. She walked on to the dockland area, passing burned out lodging houses with blackened walls, public houses with smashed windows. Men leaned against doorways smoking and watching her pass, or sat at tables outside cafes playing dominoes in the sun not noticing her at all.

In the gutter outside one of the public houses was a broken piano, its keys missing like a boxer's mouth and teetering on a fractured leg. A stool sat in front of it, as though waiting for someone to come play it. For some reason that she couldn't fathom she thought this was one of the saddest images she had ever seen. She walked quickly past.

Apart from the ruined piano and the damaged buildings and the people sweeping and cleaning everything looked normal. But she knew, from conversations at home, and from Louis wearing his army uniform everywhere to show he had fought in the war so they wouldn't shout abuse at him about the colour of his skin, that everything had changed. If you stopped for a moment you could feel it – an undercurrent of disquiet, like the imperceptible shock rippling through a forest after a tree has been felled.

A man walked past her with white robes flying behind him in the warm sea wind. A passing woman smiled at her – Irish, thought Mary, and then wondered how she knew that. Was it the cut of the cheekbones, the tilt of the head? Or maybe it was just the keening gulls overhead carrying fragments of Irish memories in their calls.

She found the Customs House where her sewing machine was to be collected and waited in line. The office was green-tiled and huge, echoing with the click-click of typewriters. She handed her note to a clerk, along with the payment. He went away and came back with her beloved machine in his arms, her Singer with its gold letters, encased in a wooden box. A label on the handle said 'Mrs M. Jordan' which gave her a jolt – she wasn't yet used to her new name.

A piece of paper stamped, and it was hers again.

Outside she stood and looked out at the shining mudflats with the sky reflected, moulded like clay by the receded sea, wooden staithes rising. Long-beaked seabirds wandered, picking their feet up carefully, tapping the mud's surface with their beaks. Beyond the mud, enormous cranes reached up into the sky, heaving and dropping their thunderous cargo, and the rigging of ships patterned the sky. And then beyond all of it, the tide, far out, just a golden line on the horizon.

A new name, a new town, she thought.

She headed for the tram stop, slowly: the machine was heavy. A tram with *TY PHOO TEA FOR INDIGESTION* in brightly coloured letters on its side clanged to a stop beside her and she made to step on.

'Excuse me.' A man appeared beside her, a very ordinary white man in a brown hat and suit, with brown glasses. 'Let me help you with that.'

And he lifted the sewing machine onto the tram, put it on a seat, tipped his hat and left. As the tram jerked away she hung onto the pole and watched him shrink until the town had swallowed him. What an ordinary man, she thought. He could have been anyone. He could even be the man who had spat at her outside the station.

And then she realised that she was now two women: the shy, pale Irish girl who ordinary men stopped to help, and the shy, pale Irish girl who was married to a 'coloured' man. And both these women were to be treated differently.

Her Singer on her lap, she sat and watched the town rattle past, her thoughts tangling in her head.

*

When she opened the front door she heard voices. In the kitchen, sitting by the range drinking tea with Ellen and Louis was an older woman, bone-thin with skin the colour of dust and deep wrinkles scribbled into her face like a child's angry drawing, and a tall, straight-backed dark-skinned young woman – a black father like Louis', Mary assumed. They were introduced as Ida and her daughter Dolly: old friends. Mary went to put her sewing machine in the lean-to, and then joined them.

The talk, of course, was of the riots and the aftermath: Jacob, whose chip shop had been firebombed, was moving back to Jamaica with his Welsh wife.

'She'll get a better welcome there than he did here,' said Ellen.

Dolly told about how she had been shouted at and pushed in the street. 'I shoved him right back,' she said, and Mary could believe it. There was a strength about her, a defiance. And she was beautiful, like a girl in a magazine – her black curly hair cut short, side-parted, clipped, and oiled, wearing a knee-length dark red dress with a dropped waist, and make-up – her lips a vibrant red and her cheeks painted dusty pink.

Mary sat a little away from them, ashamed of her long shapeless skirt and knitted cardigan.

The talk turned to old memories: Dolly told of how she and Louis used to tie string to two doorknobs, then knock on the doors and hide. The householders would open their doors only to find it mysteriously slamming in their faces when their neighbour also opened their door. Dolly laughed a loud, husky laugh, almost crying, dabbing the corners of her eyes with a handkerchief, and Louis laughed too, remembering.

'I'd have tanned your backsides if I'd caught you,' said Ida, which set Dolly off again.

'Oh, the expressions on their faces...' She waved a hand in front of her face, trying to stop herself.

Mary didn't like this woman: she's a show-off, she thought.

She imagined Louis and Dolly wandering, giggling, hiding in alleyways, and the thought made her feel sad and strange, partly because there had been no giggling or hiding in her childhood, but partly something else too. She didn't want to think of it any more so she excused herself and went upstairs.

Just like a courting couple, Louis and Mary often went out together when the house felt too full – too many voices and heartbeats, too many thoughts. They went often to the Gaiety Cinema but sometimes they just went for a walk. They had found a quiet place along one of the streams that fed the canal; a hidden shade place with a fallen tree trunk to sit on and ducks gliding in the water.

Mary decided to broach something that had been on her mind ever since she had met Dolly.

'Was Dolly your sweetheart?' she asked. Louis was looking through the lens of his camera, at the water, the leaves, at her. Click, click, click.

'Was she?'

'Was she what?'

'Your sweetheart. Dolly.'

He put down the camera carefully, wrapped it in its cloak of velvet.

'You're jealous,' he said, amused.

'I'm not.'

'You are!'

And he tickled her – jealous, jealous – and she was pushing him away giggling, stoppit stoppit...

Then: 'No, she wasn't. I never thought of her like that.'

Mary had to be satisfied with that. But she was jealous – it was a new and strange emotion, mixed with fascination and close to obsession. She realised she couldn't stop thinking about Dolly. She envied her vibrancy, her clothes, the things she and Louis shared – a history, their missing-at-sea fathers, the lovely colour of their skin. In a way, at the same time as hating the idea, she also wanted them to have been sweethearts: a beautiful couple.

It was a week later that she answered a knock at the door to find Dolly there.

'Louis is out,' she said, shortly.

'I came to see you,' said Dolly. 'D'you want a job? A girl where I work joined the pudding club so they need someone.'

Mary stared at her, at her lovely face, and realised she'd really, really wanted Dolly to have thought about her, to want to come to see her.

'I'll have to ask my husband,' she said. And then no, she thought. No: I will tell my husband.

'Yes,' she said. 'I'd love a job. Thank you.'

CHAPTER TWELVE

and alice

Dolly. Dolores Mary Davies. She was Mary's first friend since Glennie. They met by the castle every morning at dawn, Dolly always there before her, sitting on the wall and kicking her heels. Then they'd walk around the corner to the lovely imposing building of Howells the department store with its smooth, curved stone, and slip in the back door, the place hallowed and hushed as a church in the hours before the customers were allowed in, no one else around but janitors and cleaners and the seamstresses and the corridors scented with furniture polish.

Mary liked walking in with Dolly. She felt like maybe some of Dolly's gleam and glamour would rub off on her, that she would be someone a little more in focus than she felt herself to be. There was also a little astonishment that Dolly had selected her as a friend. And also, still, her feelings for Dolly were complicated: she was still jealous of her. Jealous of all the things she loved about her.

In the sewing room in the basement they, and a small group of other young women, mended, altered, and made new clothes, pinning them to a sightless mannequin and then eventually, in a special room with velvet curtains and a large ornate mirror, onto the customer themselves – usually a rich lady from out of town.

As long as the boss could see their work was being completed on time they were allowed to talk. Dolly told Mary about her fiancé, Isaac Baptiste, a seaman from St Lucia, who she hadn't seen for two years. She kept his letters, posted from all around the globe, in her purse and a photograph of him in a locket round her neck.

They would marry when he came back, and she would open her own haberdashery shop, and then there would be babies – four, she thought: two boys and two girls. She couldn't decide yet on their names.

She was always breaking into song, like Tess, and like Tess she didn't seem bothered about what people thought of her. Mary told Tess about her in letters:

'I feel so much more at home here now that I have a friend. She makes me think of you, and when I'm with her I miss you a little less. I think you will like her.'

Tess wrote back, enclosing a photograph of a young woman looking quizzically at the camera, her head to one side. Curly hair – red, Mary guessed. She had freckles. A country girl look.

'This is my friend Alice,' Tess wrote. *'I think you will like her too.'*

CHAPTER THIRTEEN

missing

There was music that had come from America and it was created by Black people.

It was called jazz.

Louis had a crumpled photograph cut from a newspaper of the Southern Syncopated Orchestra seated with their instruments in front of the grand ornate organ in Brighton Pavilion, tall bowed palm trees above their heads. They were so famous they'd even played to the King and the Prince of Wales.

'I wish I'd travelled to see them,' he said. It was too late now – nine of them had died when the ship they were on – the SS Rowan – was wrecked in a fogbank in the Irish Sea one dreadful night. The surviving members never played together after that.

But there were others who came after them. Louis saved up from his Post Office wages and bought a gramophone and some records: Louis Armstrong and Sidney Bechet, from the Syncopated Orchestra, Bessie Smith. On Sunday evenings they sat by the range and waited while Louis carefully lowered the gramophone needle till it caught in the groove, waited for the strange music to fill the room – all the crackle and grief and rhythm and beauty of it. Mary almost couldn't bear the way it moved deep inside her and propelled her out of herself at the same time, the instruments and the voices singing of loss and longing, singing about how cruel the world was: how cruel and how unbearably beautiful.

All of them became lost, all in different places on these dark evenings while the music bled into every crack and corner and shadow.

'Your father would have loved this,' Ellen sometimes said to Louis, from some faraway place in her heart.

*

Dolly's beau, Isaac Baptiste, had returned from sea and there was to be a wedding before he disappeared around the world again. This was partly pragmatism on Dolly's part – as his wife she would get part of his wages paid to her monthly, and she was saving to open her own haberdashery shop.

Mary heard her arrive, all bustle and laughter and the sing-song of her voice. Mary was in the lean-to hanging old curtains over the glass to protect their privacy. Dolly came in, clutching a brown paper package in her arms.

'Just wait till you see...' she put the package on the table and unwrapped it. Inside was a square of folded fabric which she shook out like a flag. It was rose-pink and caught sparkles of light as it moved.

'Crepe-de-chine. Isaac brought it from China.'

Mary took a corner, rolled it between her fingers, feeling its gleam.

'You're going to look like a princess.'

Dolly stripped to her underwear: a lace bandeau bra and step-ins that she had made herself. She exclaimed, laughing, against the cold and rubbed her bare arms. She is not ashamed, thought Mary, briefly.

Shame ran through Mary's veins like blood, and even her own husband had not seen her naked.

But why should Dolly feel shame? She was beautiful with her smooth brown skin, her body all shadow and curve, softness and strength. They had spent weeks in here poring over fashion magazines to find the dress they wanted. Now, Mary carefully placed the crepe-de-chine back inside its paper wrapping, shook out a roll of cotton fabric and wrapped and unwrapped pieces of it

60

around Dolly's body, pinning, unpinning, adjusting, standing back to study the effect.

'I want to be unforgettable,' said Dolly. 'When he's far away I want him to look right through all those beautiful women, and just remember me.'

'He is marrying you because you are unforgettable,' said Mary, folding the material around Dolly's hips, her belly, her breasts. From the back room came the jangly sound of Louis playing jazz on the piano.

Finally Mary was ready to cut the pattern, was ready to lay out the shimmering fabric and guide her scissors through it, was ready to guide it through the rhythmic needle of her Singer, to make Dolly's wedding dress – a rose pink dress in a bias cut with a waterfall of ruffles raining from the waist.

*

Of course, there was jazz music at the wedding, Louis on a chipped old piano, and friends of his on saxophone and drums. Noah sang with a voice like water over stone – smooth and barbed. Often in the evenings they'd meet up to play in the back room of a Maltese boarding house – Louis coming back late a little dreamy and smelling of smoke.

There had been a brief, perfunctory visit to the registry office, before convening in a smoky back room in the Red House on the river by the docks.

Dolly looked like Josephine Baker.

Isaac Baptiste was nothing like her at all – he was as quiet as she was loud, polite as she was brash. Mary felt strange watching her with her new husband: it was as though she was a stranger, hanging onto him, never letting him go, melting herself into his tall body. Mary had always known her as straight-backed and alert, watching for threat, but now she was soft, acquiescent.

Neither Isaac nor Dolly stopped smiling all night.

Ida and Ellen sat by the bar sipping sherry. None of Ida's family were there but Isaac's sister was, with her brood of exuberant children in their Sunday best who played chase between the legs of the dancing guests. Mary caught them, lined them up: what are your names? And they told her and she immediately forgot and pressed coins into their warm palms. For luck, she told them. And she wondered, will mine look like that one? Or that one?

Because Mary had a secret.

She knew the signs by now – her breasts hard and tender, her dress a little tight. She hadn't told anyone as it was Dolly's day, but maybe tomorrow she would tell Louis. She sent the children on their way and slipped outside to the privy, her ears ringing from the music.

And then she saw it. A red stain in her underwear.

She sat there a moment, just breathing. Then she stuffed newspaper into her underwear and walked down to the water, watched the hush and suck of the tide seeping against the muddy shore.

At least no one knew. She would have hated to have spoiled the day.

She could hear the music over the wind but then another noise too. A crying; something lost. She pushed her way through teasel and seagrass, her dress snagging. In the shallow mud was a canvas sack, half-submerged, tied tight shut with string. She hauled it out: something heavy weighing it down. She snatched and pulled at the string until it gave way, and peered inside.

Inside was a puppy, wet, whimpering, his eyes wide in fear.

'Ssshh, sssh.' Mary scooped him up, felt his shivering heartbeat. He was so sodden and mud-covered that she couldn't tell his breed. She wrapped her shawl around him. Shh, shh. His quivering body quieted a little as she held him.

Sssh.

She rocked him, like a child.

Her face was wet with tears: she hadn't felt them come. She put her head back and let them flow, hushing the puppy. Hushing herself. The music drifted out from the party into the pearly air, and the dockland cranes were silhouetted against the sky like strange dancers.

She wiped her face. She looked at the puppy who shivered in her arms and she thought, I lost something, and I found something.

She went back to the party, where no one noticed she'd been gone, and where everyone crowded round to look at the puppy, the children poking their small fingers at him. His ears flicked back and fore, trying to work out what was happening to him. The landlady fetched a bowl of milk and he licked it off Mary's finger with a rough pink tongue.

'A corgi, I think,' said Ellen. 'Are you keeping him?'

'Yes,' said Mary, a little defiant, expecting resistance. But Ellen said nothing, and Louis smiled and bent in to scratch the puppy's head.

'Always fancied me a dog,' he said. 'What you going to call him?'

'Reggie,' said Mary.

Reggie was the name of her father's dog, the dog they had left behind a lifetime ago.

*

It was time for the photograph. Louis set his camera on the tripod and corralled the guests into a group around Isaac and Dolly. Mary clutched the puppy against her. When Louis was happy with the composition he set the timer on the camera and ran to join them. He put his arm around Mary's shoulder and everyone fixed their faces into a smile as the camera whirred and flashed.

It was a happy photograph: everyone said so when he had developed it. No one could have guessed that there was a heartbeat missing.

A few days after the wedding Isaac went to sea again. Dolly wept at the dockside: she didn't know when she would see him again.

Mary watched them, two figures in this enormous uncaring industrial landscape, clinging onto each other, trying to be one another's anchor while knowing in a few minutes from now they would both be set adrift.

And Mary was too: adrift and insignificant as seaweed.

CHAPTER FOURTEEN

shutters

After Glennie disappeared, Mary wrapped all her feelings up and hid them away in the darkest part of herself. Like pulling the shutters down on a shop. Like putting your corns in your pocket, which is what Mother Superior told them when they said their feet hurt from the horrible charity shoes. There was no point, she decided, in loving anyone because in one way or another they always left you. She became the best orphan in the whole world, which was easy because the orphanage was the whole world. She was the best at scrubbing floors, scouring pans, emptying the nuns' chamber pots, pushing a brush down into the stinking privies.

When Mammy came to visit she was sullen and silent. I hate you, she thought to herself: I hate you because you left us here and you won't do a thing about it. A new girl was put into Glennie's bed, a girl with eyes the colour of grief and sores on her skin, and in the night Mary heard her crying and closed her eyes tight against the sound: I don't care, she thought. I don't care.

She was put in the nursery to look after the babies and she didn't care about them either – skinny little things with their reedy wails and their sour stench. She handled them roughly when she poked bottles into their mouths, when she changed their foul nappies, and she avoided their eyes. The nuns whispered that these were wicked creatures, born out of wedlock, mostly, or to mothers who were mad or bad or both, and nobody would ever care about them apart from taking care of their most basic needs, which was the Christian thing to do. Some mornings Mary came in and one was gone, so it was a good job she hadn't loved them or she wouldn't have been able to bear it.

And then one day, quite unexpectedly, everything changed.

It was an early spring day and she was sitting by the window feeding one of the babies. From here she could just see chimneys from the city in the outside world, smoke wisping into a lemony sky – the outside world that may as well have been in a far-off galaxy rather than being just beyond the wall of the vegetable patch.

'Mary Byrne, you're to come with me.' It was one of the younger nuns. Mary pulled the bottle out of the baby's mouth and put it down in one of the metal cots. The baby's wail wafted after her, sad as a bird, as she followed the nun out.

They went into Mother Superior's office and there, in a smart woollen coat and gloves and her hair freshly curled, was Mammy. Mary stared at her: was someone else dead?

Mother Superior came in looking a little flustered.

'Mithith Byrne,' she said. 'I underthtand you have come for...'

'My children,' said Mammy, peeling off her gloves. 'That is correct. Fetch them for me please. I'm taking them home.' She reached out and felt Mary's shorn hair, scratching at her scalp. Her touch felt nice, like a dream. Mother Superior made a face at the young nun, who scuttled off.

Mammy's face was pinched and angry.

'I'm afraid the children have picked up a cathe of the lithe,' said Mother Superior, watching Mammy examining Mary. 'It will thoon grow back.'

There was a strange feeling strange in Mary's stomach: she had to keep her mouth tight shut to stop it from bursting through her throat and out through her mouth in a peal of giggles.

The nun appeared again with Nora and Tess. All had chopped hair, and were thin, but Tess's cheeks were still rosy. Nora's skin was the colour of dust, and blistered.

'They look like they haven't been fed in weeks,' said Mammy.

66

'Mithith Byrne, we have taken very good care of your children while you were unable to.'

Nora stood passive as Mammy examined her hands, which were crusted with pus-filled sores.

'You call this care? You worked this child half to death and starved the others. If I could I'd take every single child away from you.'

Mother Superior raised the part of her face where her eyebrows used to be, while Mary and Tess shared thrilled glances. Nora stood there passively staring at the air in front of her face.

'Maybe you thould have thought about thith before abandoning...' said Mother Superior but Mammy interrupted, looking at the nun as though Mother Superior no longer existed.

'Fetch their things, please.' She smiled at the girls. 'We've already spent too much time here.' Mammy had brought hats to cover their awful hair, and she fixed those on as the nun went to fetch their rosaries and other small odds and ends they had accumulated: it didn't amount to much.

When they went outside the sun was dazzling – it was as though they'd been underground. There were daffodils along the path and little birds flitting. Mary started to pull the heavy wooden door behind them and stood a moment to make a promise to herself: this place is to be forgotten. When this door shuts, everything in it will be locked inside forever. She had already forgiven Mammy, had forgotten every bad thought she'd ever had about her. Because it was over.

The door slammed shut.

They walked away from the awful place, holding hands; a string of rosary beads, Mary pretending Aggie was there too, to complete the chain. And on they walked, into a new world.

*

67

They got onto a tram and sat upstairs as it jangled through the beautiful city – all the lovely hubbub and flurry of it. Tess and Mary linked arms and pointed: look at that, and that, and that; shops with bright-coloured awnings, and capped boys on bicycles, and ladies with hats, and men with walking canes, and a bag of spilled onions, and statues, and horses. Over the Liffey with the wind whipping up it and shivering its surface, dirty barges coughing plumes of smoke. Tall buildings and children running. And the cacophony of it, when all they were used to was the sound echo of silence and the sound of praying. This was like a thousand prayers, all ripped up and thrown into the air and allowed their own beautiful tangle to take shape. The world had started again, the world that had stopped like a clock when they had gone inside.

They got off the tram, squealing and clutching one another on the steep stairs, and walked along a long, straight street of terraced cottages. A woman in a scarf and apron was on her hands and knees washing her front step.

'Good morning, Mrs Walsh,' said Mammy.

'Good morning, Mrs Byrne,' said the woman, turning to squint at them all.

'These are my children,' said Mammy. 'They have been staying with relatives while I got my qualifications but they are home now.'

'Well aren't you all the pretty ones,' said Mrs Walsh, which Mary thought was very kind, considering. 'I'll be sure to come visit and find out all about you.'

Mammy beamed, turned to the children and pulled out a key from her pocket. She looked like she might burst into giggles. Then she stopped and wrapped her arms around them, her eyes wet.

'So long I've waited for this,' she whispered. 'So long.'

She opened the door next to Mrs Walsh's and stepped inside, into a cottage that smelt of wood polish and smoke and baking bread.

Like home.

CHAPTER FIFTEEN

home

In all those long nights in the cramped nursing quarters, Mammy could never sleep, despite being so tired at the end of each day that her very bones ached. Underneath her cot she had a little jar where she put a few pennies every week after paying the orphanage: she was saving for a home for herself and her children. And as she lay awake listening to the dreams of the other nurses, she imagined what that home would be like.

It would definitely have a piano, she thought.

James found one for sale in Rathgar and one warm spring day they all waited outside for it to arrive.

It was brought on a cart pulled by a black and white horse with shaggy feet as large as dinner plates. While neighbours milled around discussing how best to lift it off the cart – the cart driver was refusing to touch it – Tess grabbed Mary's hand: come on! She scrambled onto the cart, pulling Mary up with her, and opened the piano lid.

The piano had seen better days: the wood was chipped and the keys yellow as teeth, and uneven. Tess, always the showgirl, made a chord with a flourish, and nodded at Mary. They had been taught piano at the orphanage but it was as unpleasant as everything else, with their hands rapped with a stick at every wrong note.

But here there was no one to rap them. They started to play, scales and jumbled made-up tunes, the notes jarring, discordant, but beautiful and oh-so-funny. Then Tess started, very slowly, playing the top notes of *Für Elise*; she nodded Mary to play the bottom ones. Mary banged at the stiff out-of-tune keys so hard it hurt her fingers, but oh it was glorious: they passed the tune back and fore between themselves, played faster, and faster, rocking back and fore like concert pianists. The horse moved his ears back and fore to listen and the neighbours came out of their house and jostled around, and the cart man was annoyed and shaking his fist but couldn't be heard over the happy racket. And Mammy put her arm around Nora and beamed because this was it, this was home, with family and neighbours and music.

CHAPTER SIXTEEN

flowering

Mary stood in the street and watched gulls ride the air, and imagined herself up there with them: all the things she could see, the busy maze of the city and the sea beyond and then the whole world.

She was no longer the girl who imagined herself hidden, living in cracks with the spiders.

She was connected to everything now, which was beautiful and heartbreaking all at once. The city was in turmoil, sizzling with anger, workers demanding the right to unionise. Powerful employers responded by locking the men out and bringing in blackleg workers. Mary's family was luckier than many – Mammy still had her job and James was working in the Guinness factory, which didn't join the lock-out. James went to meetings and protests, coming home late at night with terrifying descriptions of police descending on the crowds with batons. Mammy, Mary and her sisters made pots of stew and took them to families who had no work now and whose children were starving, and stayed to talk and to listen awhile: the clamour for Home Rule was getting ever more urgent against the backdrop of poverty and injustice. Change, change, change, the gulls cried as they circled.

One terrible evening a slum tenement building collapsed, killing seven. The family joined the crowds of mourners who lined the streets, bare-headed, as the hearses were taken through the streets. All the blinds in the houses had been lowered for their passing and, apart from a murmur of tears the only sound was the dreadful, rhythmic creak of the carriage wheels and the hooves of the mournful horses, until they reached Glasnevin cemetery and women began keening and the mother of one of the dead tried to hurl herself into his grave, and some people in the crowd fainted. And Mary wept despite not knowing any of them, because she was woven into the city now and its stories were a part of her.

Look at me, Glennie, she thought, wanting to tell her everything. Look at me laughing at a joke over the garden wall with Molly-next-door while the sheets fly high in the smoking wind. Look at me, walking through this city of towering chimneys and dripping alleyways, a basket over my arm. Look at me walking past baskets of chickens, between the lines of sad horses in the market, stopping to feel their fragrant breath on my hand, telling them they will be all right, that someone kind will come and buy them. Look at me walking between these high limestone pillars into the indoor market and inhaling its green scent, hearing its echo. Feeling the weight of an apple, filling my basket with potatoes, turnips and cabbages, or gooseberries and currants in the summer. Look at me, wishing the stall-holders a good day, nodding at the maids of rich ladies buying heavy cuts of meat; look at the butchers with their blood-painted aprons.

It is all so ordinary, and it is all so extraordinary.

*

And then there was a war on.

Mary got a job as a seamstress in the Royal Hibernian, which everyone called the Hib, sitting in a room with ten other young women, making and mending uniforms for the boys to wear to go and fight. She tried not to think about who would be wearing them, whether they would come home again.

She liked the monotony of the work, the rhythm and purr of the machines, the whispered gossip of the women which she half-listened to but never joined in with.

James had refused to go and fight even though the Guinness factory was encouraging its employees to go to war with a Separation Allowance paid to their families. James was a fierce nationalist, refusing to accept the King's Shilling. Mammy didn't mind – with three of them working the family were managing. Anyway, given the family history, she had no great affection for the British Army and didn't want her son brought home in a box.

Nora's health didn't allow her to work and her monthly flowering was hateful, leaving her wailing in pain and vomiting into the pot they kept under the bed. Everyone knew that this was because of malnutrition and abuse in That Place but no one said anything because nothing could be done about it now. Mary and Tess sat with her on the brass bed that they shared, changed the ever-reddening cloths between her legs, laid hot towels on her stomach, and sang and read to her. They liked *Heidi* but *Ivanhoe* was their favourite – the horses and romance and battles took them flying high above Dublin, away into another world.

And meanwhile there were different battles being fought, far away but near enough to hear about them from newspaper hoardings, and see them in the cinema: all those sepia-coloured buildings reduced to skeletons: not exciting, but terrifying. Young men were mutilated and dying, like the sweetheart of Molly-next-door who now lay somewhere in a far-off land, lost to the bloodied earth. Molly carried the telegram tucked into her sleeve, folded into a tiny square so that the words were no longer legible, but were etched instead on her heart.

The war had crept to the door.

*

Look at me Glennie: I am walking in the city, giving a beggar a coin, stroking a cat on a wall. In the early morning the river still carries the night inside itself and women slosh water on doorsteps. Look at the carts with the rickety wheels rocking over cobbles and the cockle sellers with their baskets and muddy boys running in alleys and buildings with black windows like eye sockets. Taste the scent of coal fires and frying pig meat and the city at night lit up like a magic lantern. Listen to the clashing, jangling tunes of the buskers playing banjos and fiddles.

Look at me Glennie, walking home under a vast, bruised sky.

I am flowering.

*'In this world
love has no color
yet how deeply
my body
is stained by yours'*

Izumi Shikibu

CHAPTER SEVENTEEN

sweetheart

She waited in the window of the little terraced house in
Stoneybatter, just along from the market. On Saturdays farmers
brought herds of sheep past and they filled the street from wall to
wall, as far as the eye could see, calling for one other and leaving
behind little curls of fleece caught on the window ledges, and a lot
of manure for the vegetable patch.

She watched the darkening street waiting for the young man who
was, thrillingly, courting her. She had made a dress for the occasion,
carefully stitching pieces of cotton and silk late into the night, for
there was no linen or wool to be had. Sometimes her sisters poked
their heads in through the door, teasing, as she was too early, but
she couldn't wait, to slip her arm through his and feel its warmth,
to walk along the Liffey, watching idling barges and cormorants
with their wings outstretched to catch the river's shiver, and little
red-legged seabirds.

To be kissed under the clock at Clerys.

At last he appeared in the evening rain, her beautiful soldier boy,
and her hand wiped the water's breath from the window to see him
better; she always wanted to stay with this moment a little longer
before she let him in, this moment that was so full of anticipation
that maybe anything that came after it would be a little less. She had
no language for how she felt right now, watching his dark face
through the misting window, like watching someone in a film. He
laughed and gestured to the rain, asking with his hands whether she
would let him in. But he looked at her too, his rain-streaked girl,

her face blurred behind racing drops of water and the two of them savoured this, together but separated by water and glass, before she broke the spell and ran to open the door and the moment was lost in their laughter.

The day she met him she was sitting on a bench in Phoenix Park watching the lake, taking a break from work, from the rattle of the machines and the chatter of the sewing room. It was a soft day: the sun was pale and lemony and the trees were bare against a wind-whipped sky. All around were the voices of small birds. She sat near the lake where James had lost his dog Prince, who ran in after a stick, turned to look at James and then sank without trace. A heart attack, James guessed.

James trying not to cry: it was just a dog, he said. Just a dog who was under that quiet water now, bones melting into sludge.

Someone was coming: a man. A soldier. The war was over but there were plenty of servicemen around waiting to be demobilised. He had a large camera around his neck and he stopped and looked at the lake through its lens, facing a little way away from her, so that she could watch him without him noticing: some of these soldiers were fresh and you did well not to encourage them.

He was dark-skinned; maybe Indian, she thought. She watched as he handled the camera with long fingers, turning the focus this way and that. She wondered what he was looking at – the reeds bowed in the chilled air, the busy ducks, the dark ripples on the trembling water?

A thought came to her out of nowhere: look at me, she thought. Please, look at me.

He lowered the camera. She turned her head away and pretended to study the lake. She heard the heels of his boots on the path coming closer, closer...

To her disappointment, passing, walking away.

But then: 'Excuse me, miss...'

CHAPTER EIGHTEEN

a photograph

'So what did he say?'

Nora was peeling potatoes, head half turned to hear the conversation. Tess sat opposite Mary, elbows on the table, her eager face cupped in her hands.

Mary thought a moment: remembered turning to face him. Remembered eyes black as beads with a smile inside them, and the hint of curly hair under his cap. His skin: smooth, the colour of chestnuts roasting on a winter fire. His expression: a mixture of apprehension and amusement.

'He asked whether he could take my photograph.'

Nora turned fully now, wiping her hands on her apron, open-mouthed.

'Fancy that.'

Nora, with her sad pale face, was used to people looking right through her as though she was just shadow. How she would love a soldier to ask to take her photograph.

'So what did you say?'

'I said, you don't even know my name and you're asking whether you can take my photograph?'

Tess laughed.

'And he said, pardon me Miss, would you tell me your name? So I said, my name is Mary Byrne and yes you may take my photograph.'

Nora sat down, her hands over her mouth.

He'd asked her to look towards the lake, just as she'd been doing when he'd walked past.

So you *did* see me, she thought.

She looked towards the lake and felt her cheeks flush pink.

'Mary Byrne...'

As she turned back to look at him the camera clicked. He lowered it, smiled, and tipped his cap.

'Thank you.'

He turned to leave.

'But then he turned back towards me. He said, excuse me Miss Mary Byrne, may I please have your address? Otherwise how will I give you your photograph?'

'He'll never come,' said Tess. Tess didn't trust men. She was not short of suitors – this sparkling girl with her open, rosy smile – but she wasn't having any of it. 'I'm quite happy being a spinster,' she said, often. 'On the shelf suits me fine rather than having a husband to carry back from the pub every night.'

But the soldier did come. He came with the photograph of Mary sitting on the bench looking back at the camera with a coy half smile and she stared and stared at it – it was like looking at a stranger.

CHAPTER NINETEEN

a face in the crowd

The war that had seemed endless was over, and Mary had a sweetheart – a tall dark stranger, or at least a dark stranger: he was a little short. Mary was taller, and had to hunch a little to disguise it. His name was Louis. *Louis*: it seemed to Mary the loveliest name she had ever heard. And he wasn't Indian as she'd first thought, but from across the sea in Wales: his dark skin was from his father who was from an island called Barbados that Mary pretended to know when he told her, though she had to look it up in the atlas later.

He was waiting to be demobilised. He had been a sapper in France, and some clerical error had meant he had ended up in Ireland with the South Irish Horse, despite not knowing one end of a horse from the other. He wore spurs as part of his uniform which meant he had to go backwards down the stairs of the tram, which made her giggle.

Everything made her giggle in those days, her hand flying to her mouth, half-embarrassed, delighted.

Mammy liked his manners. James was initially suspicious of him; James spent most of his evenings in nationalist meetings in smoky pubs: Irish independence was coming, not before time, and a British suitor was not what he wanted for his sister. But Louis charmed him over a Guinness or two. Nora, and even Tess with her vehement anti-romance inclinations, arranged Mary's hair before every date and wanted to know every detail when she came back: the three of them tucked under the blankets in the dark, whispering and giggling

81

until Mammy yelled at them through the wall to hush up and keep it for the morning.

Louis liked watching the world through his camera and took photos of everything: Mammy and her daughters sitting in front of the piano; Tess sitting playing it late into the evening with a cigarette slowly burning between her lips; Molly-next-door posing in her doorway in her waitress uniform; James smiling, crease-eyed, through a cloud of smoke; boats on the Liffey; the tall city buildings against a tumbled sky. One day, when they were walking along the sand at Seapoint Beach, he asked if she would take her hair down. Mary had promised herself she would never cut her hair again after she had left That Place all shorn and ugly. She remembered children from the outside world putting their heads through the bars and taunting the ugly little shaven orphans. But now it fell right down her back in honey-coloured ripples, like the marks left on the shore when the tide had gone out. He watched her through his lens and photographed her hair, and neither of them spoke, and afterwards she felt as though they had shared a secret, something thrilling and maybe a little shameful.

Mary liked that there was something a little unknowable about him, a private place that he kept tight shut. The war was over but young men with haunted eyes and missing limbs begging for food in the streets showed it had been a terrible thing. Sometimes they sang mournful songs about it and you when you dropped a penny in their hats you didn't look in their eyes because what was there was something as unfathomable as the universe. But when she asked Louis about what it had been like he just smiled and said it was fine, and lifted his camera up to look at something through the lens, and she knew he would never speak about it.

They both had fathers who had died: his, a seaman, had no grave, was sleeping somewhere in the blue sea off the coast of West Africa. Louis didn't say how he had died, and Mary didn't say much about hers either, just that he was buried in a graveyard in Wicklow. Louis had followed his father to sea for a few years and worked as a ship's steward, had travelled to the far corners of the world and made friends, in the Americas, in India, whom he still exchanged letters with. But the sea-wandering had to stop, as his mother wanted him home.

On a soft spring Sunday morning after Mass, Mary packed a basket with ginger ale, roast chicken, pork pies, lettuce sandwiches and Battenberg cake and they caught a train to the sea at Kingstown. She was wearing a blue dress she had run up especially for the occasion, after Nora had pinned it onto her to adjust the fit.

The air was chilly, the colour of early primroses, full of the small, secret voices of birds. They walked to the station which was bustling and busy – lots of people having had the same idea, to go to the seaside after the long dark days of winter. As Louis held the train door open for her someone pushed in front, making her step backwards, pushing her into the body of a nun. She turned, said, 'Excuse me, sister.'

And her stomach lurched: she knew this face. There were wrinkles around the eyes now, the skin shadowed and lacklustre, but the blue was there in her irises, and the pink in her cheeks.

Mary dropped the basket.

The nun looked at Mary for the smallest moment, her eyes narrowing imperceptibly. Then she turned and moved away, her dark figure parting the crowds.

Mary stood there, the ground swaying under her feet, buffeted, a tiny creature in a vast sea. Louis picked up the basket and its scattered contents, grabbed her arm, helped her onto the train, and found them a seat in a carriage. But she stopped in the doorway, unable to breathe.

'I'll stay out here.' She stood in the corridor, pushed open the window and leaned against the frame with her eyes closed.

'May? May? What is it?' His pet name for her coming from far away, from the new world. But she had fallen through a trapdoor into the old one. She wanted nothing but to shut it all away again, to smile at her sweetheart and take his arm on this soft secret day, this blue dress spring day.

That it had happened today was unbearable.

The train started with a great shake and a shriek and rattled on its way away in clouds of stinking smoke. And Mary tried not to vomit up the bile that was rising from inside her.

They alighted at Kingstown without speaking: she could see he no longer knew what to say. It was a very ordinary day. Families strolled in their Sunday best and a band was playing from the bandstand, the tunes rising and falling in the salty air. They walked along the pier, found a bench and she sat down with the basket on her lap while he wandered to the water's edge with his camera.

She watched him. His silence, his deference, was poignant to her. He seemed so innocent, watching the horizon: he would never understand the demons who roamed the head of his honey-haired Irish girl.

She closed her eyes and saw the figure again. Tall, floating rather than walking along the edge of the pier: a beast with the face of an angel.

And Mary ran after her, pushed her and watched her fall and spin, watched her face looking up at the sky in astonishment as she entered the water, as she sank, her robes swimming around her like moon jelly. Down she went, and down, into the murk, through the reeds and shoals of fish, her arms stretched, hands snatching to find something to hold onto and save herself. Mary jumped in after her, swift and vengeful as a mermaid, felt the roar of water in her ears, dived down into the green deep. At the bottom the creature thrashed like a fish as Mary covered her beautiful, appalling face with stones and shells, with rusted chains, with weed, until she was completely covered.

And then rose to the surface. To the light.

Mary opened her eyes. There were indentations in her palms, she'd been gripping them so tight. She'd had a bad thought: she knew this. But...

'Bless me Father for I have sinned,' she said and quickly made the sign of the cross.

... but the bad thought had made her feel better.

She caught up with Louis, took his arm, smiled at him.

'I'm sorry,' she said. 'I felt ever so nauseous but I'm better now.' He was pleased, and pointed to the seals he'd been watching, and the diving cormorants, and the flocks of oystercatchers with their faraway voices, and the day was as it should be again.

CHAPTER TWENTY

portend

She dreamed that she and Louis were on the train again but this time they went all the way up the coast, back to the old cottage. They walked on the cliffs looking down at it, at washing twisting on the line and smoke curling from the chimney, at Mammy leaning on the gate with her skirt billowing against her ankles, and the little harbour boats fidgeting, the flap and jangle of them, and her sisters throwing stones into the sea. Mary, smiling, turned to look at Louis, happy to be showing him this.

But he wasn't there and she was frightened. She ran along the cliff edge, dream running, getting nowhere. Calling, calling him; staring down the cliff edge at the black rocks and the writhe of white water. Louis!

Then she saw a gravestone at the edge of the cliff, half-hidden under moss and ivy. She got down on her hands and knees and pulled at the vegetation until she could read the inscription, worn with age, barely visible. Here lies Louis Jordan.

Grief washed over her like the sea: she had lost him.

But then she saw there was another gravestone, right beside this one. Again she pulled and pulled at the ivy, wanting to see, not wanting to see. But she tugged the last tendril away.

Here lies Mary Byrne.

She woke with a shock, and all day the dream weighed on her: it had seemed significant.

The next day he arrived with his hair pomaded down and asked to speak to James and Mammy in private. They went into the kitchen and shut the door as the sisters hovered outside – Tess with her ear against the door though she couldn't hear what they were saying. When they heard the chairs in the kitchen scrape back they rushed into the front room and tried to look as though they had been there all along, though Tess was bursting to laugh, her lips squeezed tight together to try and stop it.

Mammy, James and Louis came into the room, Mammy a little wet-eyed and James standing very straight as though he felt important. Louis glanced at them, then got down on one knee in front of Mary while Tess squealed and Nora put her hand over her mouth, and before he had said anything Mary said yes.

Yes, yes, yes.

CHAPTER TWENTY-ONE

spit

She was sick on the listing mail boat on the way from Ireland to Wales, rammed up against other passengers in the hold, her face in a paper bag, Louis holding her hair back from her face. She was embarrassed at the intimacy of it; the first of many bodily secrets to be shared.

The salt-sweet air of the early morning air in the little harbour town in Wales revived her. She breathed it in as she waited for Louis to fetch their luggage, watching the hatch of train lines and the sea beyond that, with its boats and all the bustle of a little port town that she remembered from home. She had felt a little nervous at moving so far away, but this felt familiar.

Something inside of her lurched as she saw her husband approaching, pushing their luggage on a trolley. His dark, kind face was both something she felt she'd known all her life, even before any other knowing, and brand new at the same time. She still felt a fizz of excitement that he'd noticed her, chosen her. She thought it strange that the people he passed just carried on with their day, looking for their tickets, worrying what they had forgotten, chiding their children, and weren't aware of this magical man in their midst.

I will never get tired of looking at his face, she thought.

They boarded a train and found their carriage, dark polished wood and moquette seating, with faint human-shaped faded shapes on the fabric: the ghosts of other travellers. Louis put the luggage on the rack above their heads. After a lot of running footsteps and shouting and slamming of doors, the guard blew his whistle and the train belched and screeched and lurched into action, its uneven rock and rhythm transporting them to their new life.

She sat close to him, feeling his warmth, peering over his shoulder at the landscape. She was disappointed to share the carriage with other people who sat opposite them – firstly a gentleman with a newspaper, who peered over it at them when he thought they weren't looking, then a woman with a runny-nosed child who kicked at his seat constantly, and finally an elderly smiley lady in a pretty lilac hat who kept offering them pear drops they were too polite to refuse.

She wanted him to herself. They had whispered conversations – look at that, look at that. They watched the morning become yellow as the sun rose, warming the choppy sea and the little fishing villages rocking past. She wondered what Mammy and James and her sisters were doing now. The last time she'd seen them they were red-eyed, clinging to her at the dock, and she pretended to be sad too, although in reality she had been too excited for that.

The carriage became hot and breathless. Louis asked the pear drop lady whether she'd mind if he opened the window and she said no, not at all, so he pulled it down and he and Mary leaned out, her arm linked with his, watching as the train moved away from the sea and the landscape became industrial – huge smoking chimneys and black wheels against the sky and the sun made soft with dust and smoke.

At last, as the sun was at its highest, they arrived at the station at Cardiff. It was hot, but she put on her new coat so as not to crease it, and adjusted her hat. Louis pulled the trunks from the luggage rack and helped her off the train into an agitated sea of people and the train screaming at the rooftops with its steamy voice. He found a trolley and piled the luggage onto it and she held his arm tight as they pushed their way to the entrance. Hot air blew in from outside: the day felt feverish.

Just outside the station entrance stood a slightly built black man in his fifties, bow-legged and dapper, darker-skinned than Louis.

He stepped forward, his arms outstretched and held Louis for a long moment, a moment so warm and the man so tearful, that Mary thought this must be Louis' father, until she remembered.

'Uncle Noah, my wife, Mary,' Louis said, and Mary stepped forward to shyly shake the man's hand. They walked along the pavement to where a line of taxis waited in choking clouds of exhaust.

Then, Mary heard a sharp intake of breath and a rasping sound, and an ugly gob of spit landed on her gold-coloured coat, the coat that she and her sisters had spent so long choosing in Arnotts department store, the coat to start her new life in.

Louis quickly moved between her and the man, his hand on her back steering her away from the station, and she saw a look that she didn't understand exchanged between Noah and Louis. She looked back at the source of the spit, waiting for the acknowledgement of the mistake: 'I do apologise, Ma'am. I intended to spit in the gutter.' But she saw no apology, just a hard expression that looked close to hatred, belonging to a very ordinary man wearing glasses, the most ordinary man she had ever seen with his brown suit and hat and a face she would forget the moment she looked away, even if she couldn't forget the expression.

She wanted to cry.

Louis held out his arm for a taxi, and Noah caught it as though to stop him.

'Send Mary on ahead to your mother's. I got to talk to you.'

'Louis, no...' she started.

But he opened the taxi door, helped her in, and spoke to the driver, who was fixing the luggage onto the back of the car.

'Tell my mother I won't be long,' he said to Mary. He held her hand briefly, then shut the door. The driver fired up the engine and then they were chugging away through a strange town, leaving Louis and Noah behind.

This time she did cry, quietly, sniffing into a hanky.

She felt as though she had travelled to another planet, not just across the sea. Everything was strange: the streets narrower than Dublin and the buildings smaller. Then they passed a group of soldiers jostling a woman, pulling at her clothes: the taxi had to swerve to go round them. Mary stared through the back window, wondering why no one was helping, why the taxi hadn't stopped. But it was as though the driver hadn't seen it.

Sometimes her mind tilted out of its orbit. This must be what was happening now: she must have imagined the spit, the mob of hostile soldiers. She gripped at her rosary beads and breathed, and breathed, until she saw a laughing woman pushing a pram, little terraced streets that reminded her of home. A cat sleeping in a patch of sunshine on a wall.

Normal things.

The taxi stopped in front of a short row of bay-windowed terraced houses, set back a little from the road behind low stone walls and cast-iron gates.

'Are we here?'

'This was where I was told to bring you.'

The driver unloaded the trunks as trams rattled past and Mary looked around her. She was disappointed to see that on the other side of the road was a graveyard, just like the Place That Was To Be Forgotten. Louis hadn't told her this; she'd imagined that the whole of Wales looked out onto the sea.

Maybe all the way to Ireland.

At one end of the terrace was a single storey grocer shop, baskets of apples, potatoes and parsnips arranged outside. Signs on the window advertised cigars, cigarettes, tobacco and tea, and above the door was written 'Mrs E. Jordan Proprietor' and above that, under the awning was written *GROCERY – PROVISIONS* in carefully painted letters.

She took a deep intake of breath, fixed a smile on her face, and pushed open the door.

A bell tinkled her arrival into the cool darkness of the shop, slats of sunlight on the wooden floor. Behind the curved glass counter a slight woman with grey hair in a bun was holding a wire cutter over a block of cheese, looking questioningly at a young woman in a loose summer dress. A small boy stood on tippy-toes, trying to see, and in the corner a woman with painted fruit on her hat scooped potatoes from a sack into a bag.

A fly buzzed lazily over a hock of bacon.

The young woman nodded and the slight woman sliced the wire through the cheese. The woman with the painted fruit hat called over, 'You heard what's been going on at number fifteen, Ellen?'

The slight woman was Ellen. Louis' mother.

'I was just telling her,' said the young woman. 'He's not been home two minutes and she's kicked him out. He's living in the shed.'

'Give her five minutes and he'll have his feet under the table again,' said the woman with the hat. Ellen, wrapping the cheese, tut-tutted her disapproval though whether it was about the evicted man or his shed situation Mary couldn't be sure. She stood, caught in spinning ribbons of dust that gleamed in the low light from the window, wondering how to announce her arrival. This wasn't the introduction she'd imagined.

But just then Ellen looked over at her.

'I'll be with you in a minute,' she said to Mary, and looked away, but then immediately looked again and gasped and her hand flew to her mouth, and the customers turned to look too, and the child reached his hand up and tried to get the cheese now that Ellen wasn't looking, and the young woman slapped his hand.

'Mary! You're Mary. Oh...'

Then to the customer: 'Please excuse me, just a minute.'

Ellen came out from behind the counter, wiping her hands on her apron and laughing in a way that sounded like it could turn to crying any minute. She put her arms round Mary: Mary stood stiffly as she was held, tentatively put her hands on Ellen's back. She smelled of soap.

Ellen stepped back, holding Mary at arm's length.

'Oh, he said you were pretty. And tall. You're so tall!'

'My mother and father were both six foot,' said Mary. 'In Wicklow they were known as the Fine Couple. Once upon a time.'

'The fine couple...' Ellen had tears in her eyes.

She turned to the customers.

'This is my daughter-in-law! Just listen to that accent. What a lovely Irish girl.'

Then, turning back to Mary: 'Oh! But where's Louis?'

'He's gone to...' But Mary didn't know where he'd gone, and couldn't find the words to explain. She'd imagined delighting her new mother-in-law with her charm but after telling the story about her parents she couldn't think of anything else to say. Behind Ellen the staring child stuck a finger up his nose.

Ellen glanced between her customers and Mary, a childish excitement in her face, unsure of what to do next.

'Right then,' she said, gathering herself. 'You must be tired. We're next door. The door's open. You go make yourself at home – your bedroom's the one at the front,' she said to Mary. 'I'll finish up here and...'

She giggled again, girlish, looking back at her customers to share her pleasure.

'Take this,' she said, picking up a basket from beside the counter and handing it to Mary. 'I'll be in soon.'

'Thank you,' said Mary.

Ellen walked back to the counter, a little overcome, her hand over her mouth.

'And that boy of mine had better hurry up!' she called, as Mary stepped back out onto the street.

The house next door was shadowed from the afternoon sunshine and hunched, as though despondent but resigned at its position overlooking the graveyard. Mary pushed open the front door and dragged the trunks inside, then the basket.

The house inside was as dark as it had promised it would be. It smelled of damp and dust and a fly buzzed sadly somewhere. The walls were bare apart from a wooden cross with a weeping Jesus, and

94

a grimy, silent wall clock inlaid with mother-of-pearl. She left the trunks in the hall, took the basket and walked towards the door at the end of the passage, her shoes clicking on the diamond-shaped floor tiles. She pushed it open.

She saw steam, clothes hanging in front of the range, a tin bath.

And sitting in the tin bath, she saw a bearded man, naked as a bear, scrubbing at his back with a brush. She shrieked and dropped the basket: eggs shattered, potatoes rolled.

'Oh, let me help you,' the man said, looking vaguely surprised.

He stood up.

Water splashed onto the floor.

'Oh my Lord,' said Mary.

CHAPTER TWENTY-TWO

bacon

Mary sat on a worn bedspread on the bed in the front bedroom. There was a large bay window and she could see over the graveyard, and up the road, a little bit on the other side, was a public house, and down the road, backing onto the side wall of the graveyard, was a library built from smooth pale stone. Once in a while a tram rattled past.

Pink roses spun down the wallpaper on pale green stems.

She started a letter to Tess: she missed the bit out about her meeting with Ellen's brother, but she told her that the house was quite new and had an indoor lavatory and bath – which got her wondering why he was bathing in the kitchen in the first place.

She didn't tell Tess that she was alone and that she didn't know where Louis had gone.

She didn't tell about the spit. She didn't tell about how she had scrubbed and scrubbed at her new coat, but that she could not get rid of the imaginary stench of his venom: she would forever now hate that coat. She didn't tell about how she kept remembering that moment again and again, when she and the man locked eyes and she saw his naked hatred. She had travelled across the sea, to a land so close she could almost have seen from the old cottage, but which felt like another world, a world whose rules she didn't understand.

Then she didn't know what else to write. She wondered what Tess was doing now, and Nora, and Mammy, and James. Tears sprang into her eyes, hot and sharp, and she blinked them away: stop it, Mary. Stop it.

And then she heard Louis arriving home.

'I'm sorry,' Louis whispered into her hair. 'A friend needed help.'

Then Ellen took hold of him, held him as though she would never let him go. 'I thought I wouldn't see you again.' She was laughing, she was crying, her head on his chest, wiping her eyes with the back of her hand. 'That bloody war. I heard such terrible things.'

'It wasn't so bad,' said Louis. The adult part of him smiled indulgently at the top of her head, but the small boy part let himself be held, and held.

Ellen stood back, held him at arm's length. 'Still so handsome,' she said. 'But too thin.'

She turned to Mary, to include her. 'Look how thin he is.'

Louis looked around the room. 'You haven't wound my clocks.' Beside the dresser was a grandmother clock with a blue ship in its window, frozen mid-rock, and above the range, among a selection of framed photographs, was an ornate brass one. Both were silent, as though time had stopped when he'd left; as though the house was holding its breath until he returned.

'There's plenty of time for that,' said Ellen, flapping her hands to usher them all to the table. She was excited, her cheeks as flushed as a girl. Mary sat down with her new family: her husband, whom she felt she no longer knew, her mother-in-law Ellen, Ellen's brother Bright who Mary had seen much more of than she'd ever have cared to, and Uncle Noah whose relationship to the family she was unclear about. Ellen served bowls of stew, they said grace, and started eating.

The tablecloth was stained and cobwebs hung from the corners of the yellowed ceiling. The dresser, with faded blue and white plates arranged on it, had seen better days. Mary felt as though they were in a mausoleum that had been closed for years. Tomorrow, she thought, she would scrub, and sweep, and mend: she would let the light in.

She caught Louis watching her. Was he disappointed in her? She took a deep breath in: she was going to do her best.

'And what is your work?' she asked Bright, keeping her eyes fixed on his face to quell the memory of how much she had seen of him earlier.

'I travel, and I fix things,' said Bright.

'Oh, a travelling salesman?'

Ellen, unexpectedly, laughed.

'Travelling salesman my eye. He's a tramp.'

Mary looked at her, not sure whether this was a family joke: should she laugh?

'He comes home when he wants a pillow under his head and his clothes washed, isn't that right?'

'I come home when I want to see my beautiful sister,' said Bright, and Ellen rolled her eyes.

Louis asked Ellen how the shop was doing and she said it was fine though the war had had an impact which she was hoping wouldn't last. The conversation felt stilted, Ellen trying too hard. Louis and Noah didn't offer an explanation as to where they'd been and Mary felt there was something unsaid hanging in the air, something Ellen's chatter was trying to hide.

She kept her head down, stirring the watery stew round and round with her spoon, trying to look as though she was terribly hungry and needed to concentrate on it, even though she didn't feel like eating a thing. She took a spoonful.

'So, Mary, you're a Dublin girl.'

Mary had a piece of chewy bacon in her mouth. She nodded, shook her head, tried to swallow it, but it stayed.

'Mary has been living in Dublin but she was born in Wicklow,' said Louis, to help her.

'Ah. My mother was from Ireland. Galway.'

Mary nodded, smiled, tried again to swallow the offending piece of bacon.

'Best people in the world, the Irish,' said Bright, soup spitting into his whiskers.

'Good and bad everywhere,' said Ellen.

'True, very true,' said Noah.

Mary felt a little panic rise inside her, like she would be stuck here forever with everyone chatting their nonsense and her mouth stuck shut.

But then, from outside, came a loud crash, the sound of broken glass. The family froze for the smallest second and jumped up from the table.

Mary spat out the bacon and slipped it into her pocket.

Watching the moon
at midnight,
solitary, mid-sky,
I knew myself completely,
no part left out.

Izumi Shikibu

CHAPTER TWENTY-THREE

stench

She remembers it now. The shock of it: the fear.

Ellen's shop window, smashed; shiny pieces of glass everywhere. Shadowed people running into the hot night. Ellen screaming: 'Come talk to my face, you cowards. You bloody cowards.'

And later, after they had all helped to hurriedly board up the shop window, and the windows of the front room just in case, Mary lay in the brass bed beside her husband listening to the shouting outside, the distant gunshots; the town turning in on itself.

It was the first time they had slept in the same bed. She felt strange and shy, slipping into bed beside him, only the film of her nightgown, and his, between their naked skin. His warmth made her shiver a little, but they both knew that tonight they would just hold one another.

'I'm sorry,' he said, wrapping her plaited rope of hair around his hand. She put her head on his chest: his heart pumped a soft rhythm inside her.

'Why did they do it?' she whispered.

There was a long silence. She knew that he was staring into the darkness as he looped her hair through his fingers.

'Because we are different,' he said.

She still didn't understand. Then, she remembered something. She told him about the soldiers she'd seen in the street, shoving the woman, pulling at her clothes. Why, she asked.

'I expect,' he said, 'she'd married a black man.'

*

In the morning Louis and Noah announced they were going to help a friend who was in trouble, and Mary insisted on going too. She was afraid of being alone with Ellen and even more afraid in case Bright decided to take another bath.

Louis wore his South Irish Horse uniform. It was green with red stripes and shiny brass buttons.

'I served this country,' he said defensively to the taxi driver as they clambered in.

'Not my business,' said the taxi driver. 'Not anyone's business. Hooligans, that's all they are. Need to be thrown in a cell if you ask me.'

They all relaxed after that. Noah sat in the front chatting to the driver and Mary leaned her head out of the window, feeling the breeze on her face.

The taxi driver let them out in a street of shops where a small crowd of people jostled. They turned and looked at Louis, Mary and Noah: expressions of hostility. Without looking at Mary, Louis said, 'stay here.'

'I won't,' she said, standing up straight, stretching into her full height, facing the people. She took his arm, and he looked at her and gave in.

'Stay close then,' he said, and then to Noah, 'I'll go first.'

The air was thick and stinking and caught in her throat.

Louis and Mary moved forward, and the crowd, acknowledging his uniform, reluctantly parted.

'Fuck off!' someone shouted and Louis, guessing the shout was for Noah, shouted back, 'He's with me!'

In front of them was a charred shop, its windows blown out, its sign – *JACOB'S FISH AND CHIPS* – only just visible under thick smears of ash. The pavement was sparkly with broken glass and the skeletons of chairs were stacked against the wall. A black man stood in the doorway of his ruined shop. He looked at Louis but said nothing: he had no words for what had happened. Then the man – Jacob – and Noah embraced, and the crowd rippled with venom and someone shouted, 'Go back where you came from!'

Louis shouted back, 'I think it's you who'd better go back where you came from,' and Noah said, 'We sort this. We sort this,' to Jacob. His voice full of soothing.

Somewhere in the darkness in the shop behind him a woman wept. Mary stepped inside, into the stench of burned oil, and saw a white woman sitting on a stool with her head in her hands. Mary knew what it was like to lose everything, and that there was nothing that could be said. She touched the woman's arm lightly and picked up a sweeping broom.

*

'*I thought it was just in Ireland that there was trouble,*' she wrote to Tess. '*There they are fighting for workers' rights and for independence. Here – I don't know what they are fighting for. It seems all the hatred began with a picnic.*'

'A picnic!' shouted Bright in his coal-smoke voice. 'This whole bloody thing started because a group of immigrant men and their white wives went for a bloody picnic in a bloody car.' It was enough, it seemed, to explode the whole town.

The family hunkered down. Some nasty words appeared across the boards on Ellen's shop overnight and Louis went out to paint them over: apart from that everyone stayed indoors. Ellen said she wasn't opening her shop again until everything had calmed down, and when she did re-open there were certain people she would not be serving again.

Bright read aloud from the newspapers: Race riots! the headlines screamed. The police couldn't cope alone, had enlisted the military onto the streets. There was talk of guns and knives, fear of unemployment and lack of housing, of white women being seduced, and an easy answer as to who was to blame for all of this. And it

105

wasn't only the homes and businesses of black people being targeted, Bright said: Chinese laundries were being destroyed, Greek and Arab boarding houses attacked and burned.

Murder in the streets: skulls fractured, throats slashed.

"'We went to France and came back to find these foreigners have got our houses and our jobs. We've got to get rid of them.'" Bright read from the *Echo*.

'Tommyrots the lot of them,' said Ellen. 'Should have left them in the trenches.'

Mary was afraid, afraid of an angry baying mob beating their way into the house, knocking her teeth out, slitting her husband's throat, burning the house around them. She quietly worked around the family, sweeping, scrubbing, mending: making this house into a home where they could all live peacefully when all this had ended. But until then they slept with rocks beside their beds.

It did end, although no one would ever be the same again, knowing the loathing that could hide in a neighbour's heart.

And Mary could never forget the smell of Jacob's burnt chip shop.

The stench of hate.

CHAPTER TWENTY-FOUR

vagabond

Later, Bright will tell them about the day he spent on an ice-draped hillside mending fences, the spindly jag of them scrawled like an etching against a low sky. As payment he received a dish of hot mutton stew and a mug of ale which he enjoyed in a warm kitchen with sheepdogs dreaming on his feet. That night he slept in a hay barn, wrapped in his coat, the mountain wind spinning through his dreams, ice-candles suspended from the window frames.

He will tell them about rising in the still-dark morning and trudging down the mountain where sheep huddle under wind-sculpted trees, his head bent against a wind sharp enough to slice your bones, down, down to the black river.

Breathing the sulphur-scented air of Blaenrhondda, with the dark wheels of the colliery slowly spinning high above him, he clambers up the side of a coal train, covers himself with his coat and watches the pale sky burn gold as dreams, before the grey clouds hunch over again. The train rocks down the valley to Pontypridd and on down to the docks.

The mountains blue as moonstone.

In his pockets he has curious objects to give as presents: pine cones, shells, a rusted key, a corn dolly. Some years he kept to the same round-the-country route, landing in the same place in the same month where the farmers and smallholders waited for him with their lists of odd jobs. When he first started his wanderings he was running from grief, but when he realised that that is not possible however far you go, he started searching for her, his girl, looking for her in shadowed doorways and the eyes of strangers.

But he is not completely adrift – there is still a small thread left that calls him home, so when he picks up a letter from his sister to tell him of birth or death, celebration or calamity, he goes.

But this is not one of those times. He drops down from the train as it trundles its way through Cardiff. He crosses the tracks, his bag slung across his back.

It's Christmas. And at Christmas he is always home.

He pushes open the front door of Ellen's house, inhales the scent of polish and bread. He calls hello, but no one answers. The house feels oddly empty.

Except he can hear a baby crying.

Leaving his bag by the front door, he goes upstairs towards the sound, gripping the rail tight to help himself up: those icy nights have not been kind to his bones. The sound is coming from the front bedroom – a heart-wrenching wail of melancholy: a lost child.

At the end of the bed is a cot. He looks down at the baby who stares up at him, her face red raw with grief, her body shuddering. Hey, little one, he says, gathering her into his arms, pressing his cheek against her hot wet face.

'Where's your Mammy?'

He carries her downstairs and she quiets, though the sadness hasn't yet left her body which still trembles in tiny spasms of grief.

A pot steaming on the range shows that someone has been there recently, but the room is empty. But then he hears a dripping tap. He walks through to the scullery and there is Mary, looking, looking at nothing at all. Just listening.

She doesn't turn when he comes in. The sound of the tap seems to fill the whole space, punctuating the silence. Bright and the baby stare at her. Then he reaches over and touches her shoulder. She turns and slowly swims back from the place where she's been, looks at him as though through a lens.

'That tap needs fixing,' he says.

After a pause Mary nods, takes the baby from him, traces her finger across the coal dust that glitters her face.

Bright fixes the tap so it stops dripping. And this part of his journey home he does not tell.

CHAPTER TWENTY-FIVE

scratch

Mary and Ellen sit by the range making wreaths and plaits from ivy and holly, the baby sleeping in her cot between them. Ellen's aching stockinged feet warm themselves on the sleeping dog. Bright and Louis play cards at the table while Bright regales them with stories of his travels – birthing a stuck lamb, tying a drunk man to his horse to be carried home, rescuing a full line of fly-away washing from a cliff-edge. Louis listens with his faraway smile and Ellen interjects sometimes with 'goodness' or 'fancy that!' The fire in the range spits and sings and the dog half-barks sometimes in his sleep and the baby curls and uncurls her fists, clasping the dreams of her small, vast day. There are blankets rolled against the doors and windows to keep out the creep of cold and sea wind, and the sad song of the foghorn sings the town to sleep.

In the morning, which is not morning at all but frigid night, Mary rises, hating it. What other living creature would be awake now, would not be tucked in a burrow. Blowing on her fingers to warm them she fires the range, and then stands against it for a moment with her skirt hitched up to warm the back of her legs.

It is not washing day, but she has to wash Bright's clothes. Whispering secret curses to herself she soaps and scrubs the filthy garments on the washboard, noting the darns and patches she will have to do when they are dry, and puts them in the pan to boil. Outside a sad robin briefly sings into the darkness, and the Christmas goose shivers on its rope in the sliver of winter's breath that they could not completely keep out.

Ellen rubs her hands over the range, massaging her swollen fingers, putting off the moment when she will go and unlock her shop, which will be almost as cold as it is outdoors.

Mary stirs a pot of porridge that bubbles and spits like lava, and makes tea for Louis who will work late today, carrying a sack on his back heavy with the season's greetings. Then Ellen is gone, and Louis too. Mary fetches rum, brandy and a jar of sugar from the pantry and, with not too much care, pours them into a pan and sets it to bubble on the range. She finds some scraps for the dog, feeds the baby, changes the baby, wraps her in blankets and puts her in her pram on the front step. The sky, at last, is lightening, bruised lilac with a broken moon flying. Then, to the warm sounds of the kitchen and the scent of warming Christmas punch she settles by the range to pluck the goose.

Poor goose, she thinks, as she pulls, and sneezes: you thought they fed you because they loved you.

But the plucking of it is rhythmic, and her thoughts untangle and fly loose as feathers.

'Morning!' Bright, coming in wearing his big old hobnailed boots (how many times have I told him to leave those by the door, Mary wonders). Then 'Oh!' He has scented the punch. He walks over to it, his large fingers outstretched to ready to sample it, and steps on the dog, who leaps up with a yelp, knocking Bright off balance as well as the pan of punch. Mary jumps to her feet, dropping the goose into its bed of feathers, and rescues the toppling pan just in time.

'Out!' she exclaims. 'Out! Shoo!' She flaps her hands at him to usher him away. 'Fetch me some holly. Nice bunches with berries.'

Bright tips his imaginary cap and clicks his heels together, soldier style. He whistles to the dog who follows him out, and Mary stands, and breathes.

Until she hears, from the porch, the woken baby's outraged yelling.

*

112

She has collected the day: Bright's clothes fly high outside, the goose is plucked, the floor is scrubbed, and plaits of holly and ivy are lain across the mantelpiece and the shelves of the dresser. She sits with the baby on her lap, raising her up to make her smile, dancing her kicking feet on her lap like a puppet.

What does she see when she looks at me? Mary wonders.

The front door opens wide, and a fistful of frozen leaves scatter in followed by Bright and the dog. Bright smells of ale and he has no holly with him but Mary doesn't mind that as she only said that to get him out of her hair.

'It's a cold one,' he says, clomping across the floor in his thunderous boots, the tap-tap of the dog walking behind him. Both leaving little trails of mud in their wake.

'I told you...' she says. She stands up, puts the baby in his cot, who promptly starts screaming. She waves her hands at his boots. 'Leave them at the door!' She goes into the scullery to fetch water and a wire brush, to scrub it all again.

'Let me,' says Bright, his face full of sorry, but she just pushes past him: Bright with a bucket of soapy water and a brush doesn't bode well. She leaves him in the scullery with the dog, washing down boots and paws, and gets on her knees to clean.

Which is where Ellen finds her when she comes in after shutting the shop early: business is slow and the cold is gnawing at her bones. She walks in taking off her coat, and sees Mary on her knees on the floor, staring down at her legs, a bucket of soapy water beside her. Hears the baby screaming from her basket by the range.

'Mary?' Ellen moves closer. 'What is it, love?'

Mary is looking at a little jagged tear in her stockings, made with the wire brush. On her skin is a small red scratch, a tiny bubble of blood breaking the surface.

'It's just a scratch,' says Ellen, and when Mary doesn't respond, she shakes her shoulder.

Mary turns to look at her with eyes so full of fear that Ellen recoils.

113

Bright comes in from the scullery waving his clean boots. 'Look Mary, I'm putting them by the front door.' His face is rosy and beaming and his voice fragments the air. Mary wakens, rolls her eyes at Ellen.

'I've only asked him a thousand times,' she says, and Ellen laughs, relieved, and goes to put the kettle to boil.

Christmas itself is nice: they exchange small gifts of cigarettes and cotton handkerchiefs, and Mary and Ellen chatter over the cooking of the goose, and Bright bounces the baby and she tugs at his beard which makes everyone laugh. After they've eaten they stand around the piano and sing, and Mary remembers she hasn't sung for a long time. And Louis takes photographs of them all and later he will hang ribbons of negatives over the bath, the images of them pale and strange as ghosts.

CHAPTER TWENTY-SIX

angels

The baby's been cranky all morning, and now Mary holds her against her shoulder while she cooks the cabbage in a pan of water. She hates the sound the cabbage makes as it boils, like Bright when he's eating – all that slurping and splashing and food in his beard.

And when they get home from Mass the house will stink but this is what is expected of her on a Sunday. There's a piece of meat roasting in the oven too, turning hard enough to split their teeth. She realises she has never acknowledged how much she hates this ritual before, the cooking, the eating, the cleaning afterwards: there is pleasure in none of it.

'Shh shh,' she says to the baby, trying to keep irritation out of her voice. Somewhere else in the house Louis is winding all the clocks, filling the rooms with their jitterings.

The water bleeds green as bile.

As they settle in to their pew the rain starts, skirling against the glass windows, the sound blurring the Latin incantations. Mary jiggles the fussing baby on her shoulder, thinks about the last time she went to confession which was not as recent as it should have been. Because she can't find the words for her sins.

She looks at her child, who has quietened, whose head is bobbing like a nodding-head doll as she tries to focus on the stained glass windows – the pious saints with their hands and eyes upturned. The baby doesn't see them, Mary realises. The baby sees colours and shapes and raindrops running.

How lovely, she thinks, not to see the meaning of anything.

Like Mass. The baby hears voices and smells incense and feels her mother's warmth. The baby doesn't pray, or plead: when she does, she will realise the pointlessness of it all, because sisters die and people hate but she'll keep on praying and praying anyway because that's what everyone does. Week after week, that's what they do, until they die, praying for each war to be the last, for neighbours to love one another, to never ever be left alone.

Aggie bloody died, she thinks, and to her horror she hears her words spitting out of her head and echoing around the church as though she has spoken them.

Aggie bloody died!

She looks at the priest and the choristers. She looks at Ellen, who sits one side of her, and Louis, who sits the other, and waits for their reaction.

But there is none. All are lost in the worlds inside their heads: they heard nothing.

Calm yourself, Mary tells herself sternly. She closes her eyes. Bless me Father for I have sinned...

And then, over the Latin chanting and the amens of the congregation and the wailing babies and the rain on the roof, she hears her own voice again:

'Yes, you have sinned. You are wicked. Wicked! Wicked!'

A woman in a flowery scarf glances at her. Louis shifts in his seat. They heard that, thinks Mary: they heard.

'Stop your jabbering,' she thinks, but the words don't stay in her head. 'Stop your jabbering!' the voice shouts. The priest lowers his head and looks at her, just her.

With horror, she realises her thoughts are outside her head, clear for anyone and everyone to hear. She closes her eyes to shut them down but the more she tries the louder they shout – vile words, nasty words: wicked, poison, hate, kill. 'I have a heart as dark as poison!' her mind shouts, loud enough to raise the roof.

When she opens her eyes her daughter is looking at her, has seen her too.

She scrambles to her feet, and stumbles past everyone in the pew, tripping over feet, her breath in shallow panicked gasps in her throat and her head spitting like a firework. Her footsteps ricocheting around the vast space. The words keep coming: Balls! Bootlickers! Fuck! and people turn to stare, staring at the real her, the real wicked her that she keeps so hidden. Sweet, shy Mary with the honeyed hair is a monster and now everybody knows.

And God knows, too.

She needs to get herself and her baby out of here but it seems to take an age to reach the door of the church. The candles gasp as she pulls it open. She runs out into the skirling rain, turns her face upwards to it. The baby starts to wail.

The family find her crouching in the earth, the baby cockled against her chest to protect her from the storm. Louis puts his hands under her armpits to try and raise her.

'Don't touch me!' She scrambles away from him, knees sliding in mud.

And the angels scream from their stone plinths.

*

Time must have passed. Now she sits in front of the range, Louis holding handfuls of her hair and patting it dry with a towel. The house stinks of burned cabbage.

She has mud under her fingernails.

'Baby's sleeping.' Ellen, crossing the room, standing staring at Mary with her hands on her hips.

'We need to call the doctor,' Louis says.

'You want her sent to the asylum? A rest is what she needs.'

Mary thinks yes, a rest is what I need. And is thankful that this time the thoughts stay inside her head.

CHAPTER TWENTY-SEVEN

fish that fly

The days slide into one another, blurred as rain-glass. She sleeps a lot – dreamless sleeps, helped by the mugs of warm brandy Ellen brings her. Louis and the baby have been moved out of the room. She misses the warm bone and smooth muscle of him; the midnight whisperings. The pink roses on the walls spin and twist and fall like leaves and at the edge of town the sea wails its winter warnings.

Then one day she wakes with a jolt and realises that with all her nonsense she has not had her child christened, and what if she dies unbaptised: then they will both be wicked creatures and it will be all her fault.

'No one can enter the kingdom of God without being born of water and spirit.'

She waits until she is sure that the house is empty and then she creeps downstairs, through the kitchen with its coal scent. The dog slaps his tail as she walks past him but doesn't move from his warm spot in front of the range. She goes into her lean-to and gets her lace-making basket.

Enough is enough, Mary Jordan: you are making your child a christening shawl: a symbol of your maternal love and devotion.

She still sleeps a lot but when she is awake she twists and plaits and knots, weaving square after square of lace. It will be the most beautiful christening shawl you ever saw, she thinks, and when she has finished it, all will be well. As she works she hears the comings and goings of the house – the coal-men's deliveries, voices rising and falling, footsteps on tiles, the chime of a clock, the creak of a step, the slam of a door. Sometimes she hears the shrill cry of her daughter. And on she works, and on, the lacing of the thread quieting her mind.

When she sleeps now, she has started dreaming again but the dreams leave her disturbed: digging into the earth and finding Mother Superior's teeth lying in tiny coffins; a child skipping in a graveyard, her mouth open in an awful smile; a church with a crack bolting down it like lightning.

She is floating, just under the water, her seaweed hair streaming all around her. She knows the lake she lies in is dark and murky but there are stones on her eyes and she can't see.

From faraway she hears a bang: a door slamming shut, and she thrashes her tail and slowly rises, breaks the surface. The stones fall from her eyes, sink to the bottom, and she becomes human again, a human in a bed in a darkened room.

She takes a moment to shake the dream water from herself, then gets out of bed, walks across the room, pulls open the curtains. Down below, Ellen is pushing the pram across the road. She stops to manoeuvre the front wheels onto the pavement on the other side, then bends in to adjust the blankets and to say something to the baby. In the graveyard beyond the wall there are crocuses clustering around the roots of the trees and gravestones throw shadows across the grass. How long has she been asleep? Her head eddies like a goldfish bowl.

She watches as Ellen pushes the pram up the road and disappears around a corner. It's like watching a stranger.

She pulls on her dressing gown but can't find her slippers. She goes barefoot out into the dark hallway. There are no voices, just the arrhythmic tick and jangle of clocks.

She doesn't know what time it is.

Maybe Louis is at work. Maybe Bright is back on the road: there seems to be no one here. But then she smells something warm, sweet, full of spice. She walks down the stairs, feels her feet cool on the tiled floor.

He's singing to himself, Noah, as he bends over the frying pan in the kitchen: *'I'll see you in my dreams, hold you in my dreams...'*

He has a nice voice. Deep, honeyed. He is flipping a fish in a pan, the dog sitting expectantly at his feet.

He turns and smiles at her. She wonders whether this is real, or whether she is still dreaming.

'Ah. They said you were sleeping.'

'I was.'

'I just got back this morning. Fancied me a bit of good food, after all that ship-slop.'

She is not sure whether she is supposed to answer, or whether he's just talking to himself. She pulls up a chair, leans her elbows on the table.

'This like something my mother and my auntie used to make. Only they made it with flying fish.'

'Fish that fly?'

'Oh yes. They fly.'

He flips the fish deftly. Laughs.

'Bit like that. But you don't get them here. This is just an ordinary old white fish.'

Fish that fly. For some reason she thinks of Glennie, a silver girl breaking the surface of the sea.

'The laughter of the women in that kitchen,' he says. 'Loud enough to be heard the other side of the island.' He smiles, and she knows it is not the pan he is looking at, but the kitchen of his mother, dark with steam and the voices of women, scented with the food of his childhood.

She thinks about her sisters.

'You turning scrawly as a puff of smoke,' he says. 'Eat with me.'

She doesn't want to eat. Lately everything she has put in her mouth has tasted like watery grey gruel. Like the food in That Place. But she fetches plates and forks and lays two places on the table, and sits down.

He serves her fried fish and beans.

121

'You can't get all the ingredients here,' says Noah. 'Got to make do. You can't send the boy out to pick you a coconut, or a breadfruit, or a christophine. And I do miss me a mango.'

She takes a small forkful of food, and tastes warmth, and spice: it tastes of Noah's memories.

'It's good,' she says.

'They say you've not been well.'

'I just needed to rest.'

'Samuel used to suffer from the melancholy,' Noah says. She looks at the photograph of the black man on the mantelpiece. He doesn't look melancholic. His eyes are a little like Louis' – narrow with a smile just behind them.

'Wish I could have helped him,' said Noah. 'But when those thoughts came they took over his head. I tried to feed him, like I'm feeding you. But at the end, I couldn't get through to him. Not with my mind, my words, and not with my food.'

His eyes are growing milky with age.

'He was a good man,' says Noah. 'Sometimes, this world too hard for good people.'

'How did he die?' Mary asks.

'He just ... he just stopped living.'

She waits for more. But then he says, 'Oh I forgot. I got you something.'

He goes out into the hall and comes back with a jar. Inside is something red-gold, something that looks sweet.

'Guava jelly,' he says and nods, indicating for her to open it. 'My mother used to make it. Got to buy it now, when I can find it.'

She twists off the top and smells the jelly: fragrant and faraway. She dips a finger in and sucks at its sweetness.

'Thank you.'

And she knows she must write a letter.

CHAPTER TWENTY-EIGHT

sisters

'Arms up.'

Ellen slips a petticoat dress over Mary's head; it's like dressing a child, as Mary stands passive, allowing her limbs to be pushed and pulled, this way and that. Her head is floating – feels not quite attached to her body. She watches an old woman stiffly wandering the graveyard opposite, pausing to read the inscriptions on the headstones.

Ellen drops a dress over her head: blue, to welcome the spring. She stands back to admire her for a moment, as though Mary were some creation of hers.

'The same colour as your eyes,' she says.

Mary watches the woman until she's limped out of the frame of the window and disappeared. Ellen unpins her hair, which drops to below her waist, and gently untangles it with her fingers. Then she runs a hairbrush through it in long strokes, tingling Mary's scalp in a rhythm of brush and soothe. Mary can hear her breath, a little heavier now with age.

'They won't be long now,' Ellen says. Louis has gone to the station to fetch Mammy and her sisters. A squirrel scoots along the branch of an oak tree and a tram rattles past.

Ellen twists Mary's hair up and pins it. 'There.' She puts the brush back on the dressing table and rearranges Mary's pots with her quick-fingered, busy touch. She always looks so certain of everything she does, Mary thinks: there seems to be no fear in her at all.

'I wish I was brave like you,' she says, and Ellen turns to stare at her, surprised.

'Me, brave? Whatever gave you that idea?'

'You went around the world on a ship.'

Ellen laughs then.

'Oh, Mary,' she says. 'A journey is a journey whether it's round the world or in your head.' She seems about to say more but a sound outside alerts her and she leans into the window to look down. 'Oh... They're here!'

*

The kitchen is breathy with laughter, bursting at the seams as everyone jostles, hugs, peers at the baby.

'Come to Aunty Nora.'

'Come to Aunty Tess.'

Reggie's whole dog body wags in pleasure at it all, at the tumbling, broken chatter.

'I've heard so much about...'

'I've been so looking forward to...'

'Would you like a...'

'Can I take your...'

'Oh, she's just so...'

Tess giggles, keeps grabbing Mary's hand, Ellen scoops the baby into her arms and Louis collects bags from the floor. Mammy, a little overcome, peers into Teresa's amused face, touches her fingers.

'She looks so much like you,' she tells Ellen.

'D'you think so? I think she has quite the look of you about her.'

Mammy finds a chair and eases herself into it. 'That was quite the journey.'

'Right then,' says Ellen. 'Us old grandmas need to get acquainted so I suggest you young ladies go out to get a cup of tea.'

Which everyone agrees is a good idea.

The early chill has gone. Mary feels as though she has woken after sleeping through the longest winter. She slips her arm through Tess's, feels lemon sun on her face. Nora pushes the pram and can't seem to stop smiling. Their voices clamber over one another, interrupting, imitating, misunderstanding, understanding. Like a song.

They find a tea-shop in one of the arcades and sit at a round table; tinkling tea cups decorated with roses and triangle sandwiches.

Nora bounces the baby on her lap, savouring the round warmth of her. She has let it be known that she cannot have a child of her own, and also that she will never talk about it. Tess plays peep-bo across the table and the baby giggles in delight every time Tess's rosy face appears from behind her blue-gloved hands.

Nora inhales the sweet scent of her hair.

'This is a very nice place,' says Nora, and they all agree, it's a lovely place and the tea-sets are the prettiest things you ever saw.

'Are you quite better now?' asks Tess. 'We were ever so worried about you.'

Is she? She thinks she is. She is happy today, at least. And nobody is shouting inside her head.

'Do you ever think about it?' Mary asks. 'That place.'

Nora frowns.

'Oh goodness no,' says Tess, covering her face again before emerging: boo!

'Put it away in your pocket,' says Tess. 'That's what they used to say about our corns when we complained, d'you remember? Put them in your pocket. Boo!'

Nora nibbles at a jam sandwich.

'It's best to leave the past where it is,' she says. 'There's nothing we can change.'

Mary pours tea. Drops a little cube of sugar into hers, watches it soak up the liquid and dissolve. Nora's right; you can't change anything.

'So how are you finding married life, Nora?' she asks. Nora has married her English shoe-maker and lives in Worcestershire.

'Very pleasant,' says Nora. She hesitates. 'Except...'

She looks around her. Then leans in, her hand held up to her mouth.

'Flatulence.'

Mary and Tess stare at her.

'When he sleeps,' whispers Nora. 'Terrible. I feel as though the roof might blow off the house.'

Mary and Tess take this in, look at one another and start laughing, and laughing, until their stomachs hurt and their eyes are watering and still they can't stop, even though people are looking. 'Oh, oh, oh....' The baby watches them in delight. It's like a letting go, like something that was trapped has been released. Eventually they become quiet, avoiding one another's eyes in case they start up again.

'How are your new lodgings?' Nora asks Tess. Tess is working at the Irish Sweepstake at Balls Bridge and has moved into a room on the top floor of a building nearby with her friend Alice.

Mary remembers the photograph of Alice that Tess sent. She knows that Alice is more than a friend.

'It's lovely,' says Tess. 'Very convenient for work too.'

'And Alice? Does she like it?

'Yes, she seems very happy.'

Nora thoughtfully sips her tea.

'Well,' she says, 'as long as she doesn't break wind in the bed then I'm very happy for you.'

Oh, lovely Nora, thinks Mary.

And then they're all laughing again, heads back, stomachs hurting, and not caring who is looking.

126

CHAPTER TWENTY-NINE

a baptism

The bed is warm and soft with them, the sisters and Mammy – top to tail like the old days in the cottage, curlers in their hair, cold cream on their cheeks. Clothes are draped high over the armchair and the room smells of breath and talcum powder. The baby sleeps at the end of the bed in her cot and everyone's dreams tangle and dance in the darkness.

Louis has been banished to the box room again.

It is lovely and it's too much. Mary has slept fitfully and not just because she has Tess's breath in her ear and Nora's feet against her back. Something is still playing on the periphery of her mind, something bothersome that she can't reach. She slips out of bed, dresses quickly. The women snore softly, quiet as cats. Mary silently leaves the room.

Outside it is still dark with just a hint of morning and the air is sweet with birdsong. Nothing moves except the streak of a rat gliding through the shadows. She walks through the town, quiet and dreaming behind its closed curtains.

She arrives at the church. Faint light glows through the stained glass windows. She pushes open the creaking heavy wooden door and the echo ripples the silence in the vast wood and stone building. She makes the sign of the cross, lights a candle, and goes to sit in a pew. The saints watch her silently from high up in their rainbow world and the air is scented with yesterday's incense and the ghosts of wet clothes.

She listens to her breath, and the breath of the building.

She had thought, sitting in the silence, she might be able to untangle the threads of her thoughts, but they are knotted so tight she can't reach their core.

It's not confession time but maybe someone will come. She goes to the confession box at the side of the church, settles herself, and after a while she hears footsteps approaching along the stone floor. The rush of a priest's habit. A shadow appears through the grill. She makes the sign of the cross.

'Bless me father for I have sinned. It's been nine months since my last confession.'

She hears a man's cough, feels him waiting.

And again she can't find the words. How to say, I can't love my child.

She remembers the darkness in a church in Wicklow, the shadows in Father Patrick's eyes as he refused to help her mother on that dreadful night. She remembers Mother Superior's pink face, always looking upwards, never down, never looking at her. She knew, she thinks suddenly: Mother Superior knew what was done to the children. She knew and she did nothing.

And then she remembers a nun's wraith-like face watching her, silent, and the drip of water.

She looks at the dark silhouette of the priest's face. A man. Just a man. He is not God.

They are not God.

'Sorry,' she mumbles. She gets to her feet, hurries away down the aisle. At the door she briefly curtsies, makes the sign of the cross and leaves.

The sun has risen, low and blinding, and she is crying.

She doesn't want to go home yet, doesn't want her sisters asking why, what. She walks along the canal, along the bank of the feeder stream, to hers and Louis' secret place. Reflected morning light shivers in the water. She sits on the bank, blows her nose, and then dips her hands into the water and drips it down her face; it's cold, and makes her gasp. It's lovely. Again she does it, and again, the sweet water running down her face, and she feels something washing away.

And then she hears footsteps approaching on the path, and someone appears.

Mammy.

Mary scrambles to her feet. 'I'm not doing anything stupid...'

'I know.' Mammy sits stiffly down on the fallen trunk. Her bones ache and creak now in the mornings – all those long shifts pacing the stone floor of the hospital taking their toll.

Mary sits down beside her, leaving space between them.

'How did you know where I was?'

'I followed you. I couldn't sleep either. It's like lying in a stableful of mules.'

Mary laughs.

They watch as a family of ducks glides past, leaving traces of themselves behind them in the water.

'D'you remember the food parcels?' Mammy asks. And Mary does: delivering food to families who lived in derelict buildings, packed into tiny, filthy rooms. She remembers the children barefoot among the broken glass and rubble. The strange smell of them, as though they lived underground.

'That's why I sent you to the orphanage. Because that would have been us.'

Mary looks at her mother and realises she has wanted to say this for a long time, and that she wants to say more too, but will never find the words.

'You always did the best for us Mammy,' she says.

Mammy sighs, stands stiffly up.

'Come on,' she says. 'Those sisters of yours will be wondering where we are.'

CHAPTER THIRTY

a christening

The lace shawl she made is a disaster: what was she thinking? It's like something Glennie might have made – a patchwork of nonsense made by a madwoman. Thank goodness Mammy has come to the rescue, bringing an old shawl from Ireland, the one all her children were christened in.

She feels disconnected all through the christening though it is nice to be with her family in their Sunday best, and to hear her daughter's name: Teresa Agnes Jordan. 'Teresa Agnes Jordan, I baptise you in the name of the Father, and of the Son, and of the Holy Spirit.' Teresa shivers in shock and then screams as holy water is cupped over her head, and Mary feels a strange feeling inside as though her insides have constricted: a primal feeling that she doesn't recognise.

Father Francis anoints Teresa Agnes Jordan with holy oil. Again, Mary thinks, as she often thinks these days, that he is just a man, that he is distracted and thinking what to have for supper, and that this is not the epiphany she had wanted it to be.

But it's lovely, everyone says so as they step outside into the late spring sunshine, as they stand waiting for Louis to set up his tripod and screw his camera on top, while they wait for him to run around to join them as the camera whirrs, counting down.

They fix smiles on their faces.

Click.

They turn to Mary: wasn't that lovely?

But Mary has forgotten this day already. It needed to be done but it was not what she wanted.

But what does she want? Where has she always been happiest?

CHAPTER THIRTY-ONE

fish and chips at sundown

The next day everyone clambers into Louis' green Baby Austin – the bathtub on wheels as Ellen calls it – to go to the seaside, Noah in the front with Ellen on his lap, the sisters, the baby and Reggie squashed in a giggly jumble in the back.

Everyone apart from Mammy that is, who, after her ride from the station, announced that until she was ready to meet her maker she would not be driven by Louis again. She is to travel by train with Dolly and Ida.

The car is Louis' pride and joy and he drives fast, way over the 20 mile an hour speed limit, ignoring Mary's protests, showing off a little. Everyone holds onto their hats as the little tin car rocks along the winding road and Reggie the dog's ears fly, his head up, drinking the wind.

It's a warm day: families stroll along the promenade and the air smells of salt. In the fairground people are hurled down the rollercoaster like puppets, limbs flying, their screams flung high into the sky. Painted horses with glazed eyes spin round and round, delighted children on their backs, and discordant organ music plays. They wait at the station for Mammy, Dolly and Ida. Dolly arrives carrying a bag: 'I have a surprise.'

'We'll come and find you,' she says, her eyes thrilled with her secret, and while the rest of them head to the beach, the grandmothers taking turns to carry the baby who is becoming heavy now, Dolly takes Mary, Tess and Nora to a little painted beach hut and they all squeeze inside and shut the door.

Dolly opens the bag, reaches inside and holds up a garment, navy blue with cream lacing around the bodice.

She's made sea dresses, just like the ones in the magazines.

'Everybody's buying them,' she says, 'so I made extra.' She throws one at each of the women.

'Oh no,' says Nora, blushing. 'The very idea.'

Mary holds it up: it's beautifully made with delicate, precise stitching. But she can't wear this.

'You can keep your stockings on if you like,' says Dolly, slightly disappointed at the muted response. 'Go on, just try it on.'

Mary looks at her, the excitement draining from her face.

'I'll try it,' she says.

Mary turns her back to them and Nora helps her undress and there's a giggle of zips and buttons as they put on the dresses. They look suddenly so different – not like themselves at all. A little less hidden.

'You like them?' asks Dolly.

'I love them,' says Tess, hands on hips, looking down at her lovely self. Nora bustles around picking up the discarded clothes.

'Come on then,' says Dolly, taking Mary's hand. But Mary pulls away. 'No.'

Walking past the crowds of people, wearing this? No. She takes her dress from Nora and slips it over her head.

No.

So it is just Dolly and Tess wearing the sea dresses when they all walk down the beach and find the others, laying the blanket out near to the shore, the dog racing round them in utter joy, digging holes, and scattering clouds of sand.

Mammy tries hard to hide her disapproval at Tess and Dolly's costumes, but Ida says, 'If I was twenty years younger I'd have me one of those,' and Ellen admires the neat stitching. Louis looks a little embarrassed but Noah says, 'Well, I think you look very nice,' and opens a bottle of rum and holds it up: 'Here's to all of us.' And everyone realises that today is somehow extraordinary, all of them together, and they all laugh.

Tess and Dolly run to the shore, crouch, dip their hands into the ice-warm brine. 'Give me some of that,' says Ellen and Noah pours some rum into her lemonade. She cups her hand over her eyes, watching the sea and the young women leaping. Louis raises Teresa up into the air, up to the sun. 'You shall have a fishy on a little dishy,' he sings: 'Dance to your Daddy.'

A few feet away, a couple sit on deckchairs. The man is reading a newspaper, but the woman is staring, not at Tess and Dolly in their sea dresses, but at the picnic gathering: Mary and Louis, Ellen and Noah, Nora, Ida, Mammy, and baby Teresa. Mary smiles at her.

The woman doesn't smile back.

'They're everywhere,' she says, to her husband, but loud enough for Mary to hear. 'Disgusting.'

She is looking at Noah, at Louis, and then at Dolly, standing on the shore with Tess.

Mary remembers the spit of that first day. Remembers Ellen cleaning ugly words off the shop front. Remembers the stench of burnt oil.

She turns to Louis, who is leaning back on his elbows talking to Noah, Teresa balanced on his knees. He holds the baby's hands, and watches the sun hanging over the sea, and asks Noah, what time is it in Australia now? What time is it in Barbados? Mary feels annoyed at his otherworldliness – why is he still thinking his cloud-like thoughts when they are being insulted?

Then she notices he has angled himself so that he is facing a little away from the staring woman. And she realises, with a heaviness, that he did hear, that he has been dealing with people like this his whole life.

Then: 'And to bring a child like that into the world. Wicked.'

The woman is glaring at Mary's child now, as she shrieks and giggles, bouncing on her father's knee.

A little spark of anger bursts inside Mary.

Mary takes Teresa out of Louis' arms and carries her down to the water, to join Tess and Dolly. Forget that stupid woman, forget that stupid woman, she thinks, but it has darkened the day.

A bird swoops along the horizon and the baby reaches out a fat brown fist, as though she could catch it. Tess takes her from Mary, dangles her toes in the froth of the waves, and Teresa squeals her delight.

Mary breathes, the sea air blowing through her head, leaving her mind clean, clear.

Wicked.

And she suddenly knows, with absolute clarity, that it isn't she who is wicked; it isn't she who is dirty inside.

On the first night in the orphanage, Sister Angelica pushed open the wooden door and they entered a dark room that sounded like water. Lead pipes ran across the ceiling and down the walls and taps drip-dripped. Sister Angelica turned to her and smiled.

'Do you know why you're here?'

Mary shook her head.

'It's because your mother is a very wicked woman.'

'No, she isn't, it wasn't her fault...'

'She's a whore.' Sister Angelica said the word slowly, lovingly, as though she was tasting it.

Mary didn't know what a whore was, but she was pretty sure her mother wasn't one. She shook her head again.

'She's going to be a nurse.'

The slap across her cheek was unexpected, knocking her backwards. She stared at Sister Angelica's lovely face, unsure of what was happening.

'I am telling you. Your mother is a wicked woman. You have come here to ensure you do not follow in her footsteps.'

Her cheeks pink as petals.

'Get undressed.'

Now, Mary watches the light play on the water, hears her daughter's giggles and the women's chatter, and the waves, and the seabirds. For the first time, she doesn't push the memory away but allows it to come, riding on the sea breeze. Spinning in the eddies.

Mary kept her eyes on Sister Angelica's face as she slowly peeled off each item of clothing, until she was naked, shivering, covering herself with her hands. Sister Angelica's eyes were no longer pretty; they were the colour of lead, gurgling with venom.

Sister Angelica grabbed her arm, threw her against the cold tiled wall and turned the tap on. Icy water flooded over her and she started to scream, but she couldn't hear her voice over the drench of it.

The door opened and the ghost nun who had taken her sisters came in. Mary looked at her through the curtain of water: now it would stop.

But the ghost nun stood in the shadows and watched.

Watched as Sister Angelica picked up a wire brush.

Watched as she scrubbed at Mary's naked body. Words spat from her mouth 'filthy-wicked-evil-sinful-dirty. Dirty. Dirty.' Water flooded down Sister Angelica's face, soaking her habit: her face was frenzied and excited. Blood sprang in small bubbles to the surface of Mary's skin and flowed, and ran, curling down the drain. Sister Angelica rammed the brush up between her legs: filthy-filthy-filthy. Mary was fighting, kicking, pushing at Sister Angelica but she may as well have been pushing at a statue: Sister Angelica was powerful, and practiced.

And all the time the ghost nun watched from the shadows.

The pain was like nothing she'd ever experienced. But the pain inside her was even worse. She deserved this. She was wicked, dirty. God hated her. She was going to burn in hell. When it was over she slumped on the floor, her little ribbed body blue with the cold and bleeding. A wicked little girl.

Only she wasn't, she thinks now. She was a child; how could a child be bad? She looks at her daughter, happy in Tess's arms, and for the first time since the birth she feels something that isn't fear.

Dolly rubs her arms. 'I'm freezing!' And they go back to join the family, sitting down on the blanket, Dolly and Tess wrapping cardigans around themselves to warm up.

Bright comes trundling over the sand pushing his rusting bicycle.

A jangle of iron pans hang off the handlebars and wrapped around his neck is a knot of coloured fishing rope. He looks like a bedraggled member of some otherworldly circus.

'Glorious day!' he shouts and Louis, who had been dozing, raises his hat from his face briefly, and Noah hands him the rum. He drops his bike on the sand, tips his hat to the staring woman, sits down next to Noah and takes a long glug of rum, drinking it easy as if it was water.

He raises the bottle: 'To your health Teresa Agnes Jordan.'

The woman is still staring. She has sunglasses on now and she is peering over the top of them at the baby. At Mary's daughter, this child who loves watching birds and shadows and leaves, who giggles at the dog, who is learning that using her voice is fun. Who thinks the whole world is a beautiful thing, and Mary suddenly feels her heart swell and break that this child knows nothing of the evil things that can live inside a heart.

Mary approaches the woman.

'Madam, may I ask what your problem is? My family and I are just enjoying a day out and not being a bother to anyone.' She speaks quietly so her family don't hear her.

The woman flushes, taken aback. She looks at her husband for support but there is nothing of him but a hat poking out from behind a newspaper.

'You are a very pretty woman,' says Mary, and the woman's hand shoots up to pat her hair, confused, pleased.

'But you are ugly inside. Which my baby daughter isn't. Which none of us are.'

'Oh, how rude. Terence…'

She pokes him on the knee.

'Terence, do something. You can't let someone speak to me like that. Especially not one of them.'

Terence grunts from behind his newspaper.

'Do you go to church?' Mary asks.

'None of your business,' snaps the woman.

138

'I think you do,' says Mary. 'I think you go to church and think you're forgiven everything, but if I were you I'd have a long look into that soul of yours, because it is full of filth.'

The woman stares back at her, open-mouthed. Mary gives her an empty-eyed, dismissive smile, just like the smile that has been given to her so many times. She enjoys the moment for a breath or two, then turns her back and goes back to her family.

She sits down on the rug, next to Louis; breathes. She can't believe what she just said to that horrible woman.

She's elated.

There is a debate going on, whether everyone should take off their stockings and go into the sea, as Dolly wants them to. Ida says they'll catch their death. Mammy says it isn't proper. Tess says she couldn't give a fig about what is proper, and grabs at Nora's arm, who is uncertain but ready to be persuaded. Noah jokes that he has no stockings to take off but is happy to sit here and look after the bags. Bright is asleep with his hat over his face and Louis is looking at the world through his camera.

'In Barbados,' says Ellen, 'they call it a sea-bath, and I think you should all go and have one.'

In this family, when Ellen speaks it means something. There is a scramble of hopping and rolling off of stockings. Toes wiggling in warm sand. Dolly, Tess and Nora run towards the sea, whooping with delight. Then Ellen too rolls off her stockings, ignoring the tuts of Mammy and the concerned look of Ida.

'Come on,' Ellen says, pulling them to their feet. 'It's said to be good for your health.'

She and Noah share a smile. 'You too.' She plucks the baby from his lap where she's been pulling at his ears and nose, kicks Bright awake, and she, Noah and Bright, Mammy and Ida follow the others to the sea.

Mary turns to Louis: 'Look.' And she slips her dress over her head and stands up in her sea dress, no longer caring about anyone else looking at her. Just him. Cool sea-breath shivers her skin.

He grins and gets to his feet, twirls her round. 'You look very pretty,' he whispers into her hair. His breath is warm, and she giggles, and it feels like the old days back in Ireland when everything was ahead of them.

Mary looks at the family on the shoreline.

'A photograph of us,' she says. 'Please.'

The outraged woman is marching back up the beach, her husband dragging deckchairs and trailing behind her. She glances back and Mary gives her a wave.

Then she sees the lace shawl she made in her bag: for some reason she brought it.

She takes it out and runs to join the others. She dips her toes in the water, feels it breathily cold, then warm. She watches the others, their silhouettes against the reddening sky, their reflections fragmented. Ellen paddles in the shallows, lifting Teresa up as the waves come, as though each one is enormous. Mammy and Ida say 'ooh!' to one another at the lovely, unfamiliar feeling of the sea sucking around their toes. Noah laughs, his trousers rolled up, his legs thin as a gull's, and Bright hasn't bothered to roll anything up, is wading, is soaked, grinning at the sky. The dog races back and fore in a frenzy of joy, his mouth snap-snapping at the waves. Louis digs the legs of his tripod into sand, moving it this way and that to straighten it.

Mary shakes the shawl out.

There had been no pattern. There are ferns, and faces, and flowers, and shells, and seahorses, and mermaids, spider webs, a running dog – a random patchwork of shapes that she had made during those dark, aching nights. A nonsense shawl. The dropping sun splinters and shines through it. She flies it in the air like a kite, like a bird, above Teresa's head, and her baby daughter snatches at the air to try and catch it.

'For you,' Mary says.

'Photograph!' calls Louis, setting the camera.

They group together as he runs to join them, smiling, Dolly and

Tess standing sideways as though they are in a magazine, and just before the camera clicks an unexpectedly large wave hits them from behind, so this photograph will have real laughter in it.

And when they look at it later they will see something strange, a trick of the light: at the edge of the laughing raggle-taggle family you could swear there were two more figures there – two small girls, one dark and silhouetted and one sunlit and silver, both blurred with sea-light.

But for now they all run shivering back to the blanket to warm themselves up and Louis brings them fish and chips wrapped in newspaper and Reggie sits begging for scraps with his face wide in a dog-smile. And they all huddle together on the beach and watch the sun drop down into another part of the world.

Acknowledgements

Thank you as always to my family: to my father Peter for his library of memories, my partner Poli for managing the chaos and for his genius in making furniture from discarded pallets, and my children, Cai, Coyan and Llaima Mali for almost never showing irritation at my questions. Thank you too to my grandmother Mary whom I barely knew as a child, and who I rediscovered in the writing of this book. And to my little grandaughter Rayén, for reminding me that life is a circular thing.

Writing can be a lonely pursuit: thank you to my wonderful writing network – Clare Potter, Louise Walsh, Rebecca Parfitt and Rhian Elizabeth – for the fun, the tears, and the constant support: I don't know where I'd be without you.

To Fizzy Oppé for her precious friendship.

While I was writing this book I moved to the beautiful Garw Valley. Rhian Bevan welcomed me and, with her lovely Newfoundland dogs Otto and Betty, took me on adventures to explore it whenever I needed a break: thank you for the chat, the laughter, and the endless mud.

Thank you as well to my dogs, Raffi, Layla and Sula, who force me to be still, to listen, to breathe, and who remind me that life is short.

Thank you to everyone at Gwasg Honno: your enthusiasm and support has been invaluable.

And last, but never least, thank you to Rebecca F. John, my wonderful editor, who once again has taken such good care of me and my work.

The Izumi Shikibu poems I have used are from *The Ink Dark Moon, Love Poems by Ono no Komachi and Izumi Shikibu, Women of the Ancient Court of Japan*, translated by Jane Hirshfield with Mariko Aratani, published by Vintage Books.

Lace was written with the support of an Author's Advance Award from the Books Council of Wales.

144

ABOUT HONNO

Honno Welsh Women's Press was set up in 1986 by a group of women who felt strongly that women in Wales needed wider opportunities to see their writing in print and to become involved in the publishing process. Our aim is to develop the writing talents of women in Wales, give them new and exciting opportunities to see their work published and often to give them their first 'break' as a writer.

Honno is registered as a community co-operative. Any profit that Honno makes is invested in the publishing programme. Women from Wales and around the world have expressed their support for Honno. Each supporter has a vote at the Annual General Meeting. For more information and to buy our publications, please visit our website www.honno.co.uk or email us on post@honno.co.uk.

Honno
D41, Hugh Owen Building,
Aberystwyth University,
Aberystwyth,
Ceredigion,
SY23 3DY.

We are very grateful for the support of all our Honno Friends.